MASON DIXON

BASKETBALL DISASTERS

Don't miss

MASON DIXON'S

other ~~disasters~~ adventures!

- MASON DIXON: PET DISASTERS
- MASON DIXON: FOURTH-GRADE DISASTERS

MASON DIXON

BASKETBALL DISASTERS

3

CLAUDIA MILLS

ILLUSTRATED BY GUY FRANCIS

A Yearling Book

Text copyright © 2012 by Claudia Mills
Cover art and interior illustrations copyright © 2012 by Guy Francis

All rights reserved. Published in the United States by Yearling, an imprint of Random House Children's Books, a division of Random House, Inc., New York. Originally published in hardcover in the United States by Alfred A. Knopf, an imprint of Random House Children's Books, New York, in 2012.

Yearling and the jumping horse design are registered trademarks of Random House, Inc.

Visit us on the Web! randomhouse.com/kids

Educators and librarians, for a variety of teaching tools, visit us at RHTeachersLibrarians.com

The Library of Congress has cataloged the hardcover edition of this work as follows:
Mills, Claudia.
Mason Dixon : basketball disasters / by Claudia Mills.
p. cm.
Summary: Fourth-grader Mason struggles to enjoy playing basketball after his best friend persuades him to join a team, and learns that the dog-hating lady next door is not so bad after all.
ISBN 978-0-375-86875-7 (trade) — ISBN 978-0-375-96875-4 (lib. bdg.) —
ISBN 978-0-375-89960-7 (ebook)
[1. Basketball—Fiction. 2. Sportsmanship—Fiction. 3. Neighbors—Fiction. 4. Dogs—Fiction.
5. Schools—Fiction.] I. Title. II. Title: Basketball disasters.
PZ7.M63963Mad 2012
[Fic]—dc23
2011014249

ISBN 978-0-375-87276-1 (pbk.)

Printed in the United States of America
10 9 8 7 6 5 4 3 2 1

First Yearling Edition 2013

Random House Children's Books supports the First Amendment and celebrates the right to read.

To Ella and Graham Morris

1

On the Plainfield Elementary School playground, Mason Dixon watched from a safe distance as his best friend, Brody Baxter, aimed his basketball at the hoop.

At least Mason had thought it was a safe distance.

The ball struck the front of the rim and shot back directly toward Mason's head.

"Watch out!" Brody shouted.

Mason watched, but didn't exactly watch *out*. Instead, he stared with horrified fascination as the ball zoomed toward him. Then, a split second before it would have knocked him to the blacktop—"Fourth-Grade Boy Killed on Basketball Court"—he made a saving catch.

Mason's golden retriever—named Dog, short for Dog of Greatness—gave an appreciative bark as

Mason tossed the basketball back to Brody. Then Dog gave another appreciative bark as Brody caught it. Dog lived at Mason's house, because Brody's dad was desperately allergic to all furry pets, but both boys shared Dog and loved him equally.

"Hey, Mason," Brody said, practically dancing as he dribbled in place beneath the hoop. "You're good! You have quick reflexes!"

Well, yes, sometimes a person's reflexes became surprisingly good when the person was facing impending death-by-basketball.

"Come on, Mason, shoot some with me. Dog, you can come and shoot some, too."

Dog wagged his tail at the sound of his name. Besides, Dog loved playing with a ball, any ball. Despite having only three legs, Dog thought that retrieving balls, or sticks—or any tossed object—was life's greatest joy.

This was one way in which Mason and Dog were different.

"Did I tell you I talked to my parents?" Brody asked. "I told them I want to try basketball at the YMCA for a season."

Mason would have guessed this without Brody telling him anything. Of course, Brody would want to try basketball. Brody was interested in trying everything. He was finishing up a short soccer season right now; he'd play baseball in the spring. Why not play basketball, too?

That was one way in which Mason and Brody were different.

It was almost evening, on a mid-October Friday, and the Plainfield Elementary playground was deserted, except for Mason, Brody, and Dog. Neither boy had a basketball hoop on his garage, so this was the perfect place for playing basketball.

If any place was a perfect place for playing basketball.

Mason edged slowly onto the court. Brody took a few more dribbles, and then shot again, and missed again.

"Get the rebound!" Brody called to Mason.

Mason managed to stumble after the ball and grab it before it rolled off into the long grass at the edge of the blacktop. He knew the basic idea of how to play basketball, from playing it for a few weeks each year in P.E., but he had never been good at it, or good at any sport, for that matter.

"Now shoot!"

Without bothering to take careful aim, Mason tossed the ball in the general direction of the hoop.

"You're not even trying," Brody scolded. He tossed the ball back to Mason.

This time Mason studied the distance to the hoop before releasing the ball. His eyes widened with disbelief as, without even grazing the rim, the ball sailed neatly through the hoop and into Brody's waiting hands.

Brody cheered. Mason continued to stare at the hoop.

"Besides, you're tall," Brody said as he hugged the ball to his chest. "You'd be good at basketball because you're tall."

People often said that to Mason, that he'd be good at basketball because he was tall. They seemed to be forgetting that basketball involved a few other things besides height, such as skill in shooting, passing, dribbling, and guarding. Little things like that.

"I know I'm short," Brody said as he began

dribbling the ball in slow circles around Mason, "but that can be an advantage in basketball."

Mason didn't say it, but he couldn't help thinking: *Then why are so many professional basketball players seven feet tall?*

"A short guy can dart in and out, and the tall guys won't even know what's coming at them."

Brody assumed a crouching position, as if to block an opponent's shot.

"But you know the real reason why I'm going to be good at basketball?" Brody asked Mason.

Mason knew Brody wasn't really bragging. Brody was just so in love with the idea of playing basketball for the first time, and being good at it, *great* at it, that his enthusiasm bubbled out of him like happy steam from a singing teakettle.

"Why?" Mason asked, because Brody was clearly expecting him to.

"Because I have *hustle*," Brody said. "I do. I have hustle."

Something Mason decidedly didn't have. And never would have.

"Look," Brody said as he shot again. This time the

ball teetered on the rim and then dropped in. "If you sign up for the team with me, then I'll have a ride to all the practices and the games if I need one."

"What about your parents? Why can't they drive you?"

"They told me I'm already doing too many sports this year, and Cammie and Cara are playing basketball, too, and it's their only sport this year, and so they get priority. That's what they said."

Mason let Brody bounce-pass the ball to him, and he took another shot. This time he felt a strange satisfaction in missing, as if his wide shot proved Brody wrong about Mason's supposedly great potential as a tall player with quick reflexes.

"Um, Brody?" Mason apparently needed to remind him. "I'm not what you would call a sports person."

"That's like what you said when we got Dog, remember? That you weren't a pet person? And now you love Dog."

Mason tried to hide his scowl. He hated being reminded that he had agreed to adopt Dog a few months ago only because of Brody's begging and pleading.

"And then you said you didn't want to be in the

Plainfield Platters, remember? You said you weren't a singing person?"

The Platters were the fourth- and fifth-grade choir at Mason and Brody's school. Mason had joined it this year, against his will, and he had to admit that it hadn't been terrible so far. He and Brody had even sung a solo together at the last concert.

Brody went on. "Mason, I really think my parents mean it this time, that I have too many activities and they're not going to drive me to this one."

Mason cast about for another way Brody could get his rides. "Does Sheng want to play basketball? Or Julio? Or Alastair?"

Sheng was Brody's second-best friend. Julio was Brody's third-best friend. Alastair was Brody's fourth-best friend.

Brody shook his head for each name. "Either they're already on another team, or they don't want to play basketball."

"But I don't want to play basketball, either!"

Somehow Mason had already lost the battle.

"Believe me," Brody said happily, "this is going to be great!"

Mason sighed.

At breakfast the next morning, Mason knew that he would have to tell his parents that they needed to sign him up for basketball; Brody had said that if they were going to enroll for the fall season, they needed to register right away.

Mason didn't think he could stand to hear how happy this was going to make his mother, who was always after him to try some supposedly wonderful new thing: to eat a food like sushi instead of macaroni and cheese, to wear something other than solid-colored T-shirts and brown socks.

She had been the one who had most wanted him to get a pet.

She had been the one who had most wanted him to join the Platters.

And just the other day, she had been after him to do a team sport. She had read in one of her parenting magazines that kids who didn't do a team sport by age ten never ended up doing a team sport for the rest of their lives. She had acted as if this was a terrible thing.

Mason took the first spoonful of his plain Cheerios and milk. He looked over at his mother, who had just fixed herself a plate of scrambled veggies and tofu, and at his father, who was busy doing a sudoku puzzle in the morning paper. Mason's dad was very bad at sudoku puzzles, but he had read a magazine article that said it was important to use all the different parts of your brain on a regular basis so that you wouldn't lose mental functioning as you aged. Mason thought both of his parents got too many ideas from magazines.

Given that his dad was only forty, Mason didn't think he needed to worry about warding off senility quite yet. Still, his dad squinted down at the puzzle, scowling at the little boxes in their little rows.

"I thought for sure a nine went here," he said sadly,

using his pencil eraser for the twentieth time in five minutes.

"Um, Mom and Dad?" Mason said. He hated to interrupt them, but it was now or never. He tried to keep his tone light and casual. "I was thinking that I might go out for basketball this year."

His father laid down his pencil.

His mother set down her fork.

Oh, Mason, that's wonderful! Oh, Mason, we're so proud of you!

His mother found her voice first. "But, Mason."

But, Mason?

"You've always said you're not a sports person."

If there was anything irritating, it was hearing quotes from your previous self.

"Sometimes people change" was all that Mason said in reply.

"But—basketball? Dan, isn't that a very *physical* sport?"

Mason's dad still looked stunned. Finally he said, "At least you're tall. That's something."

"*And* I have quick reflexes," Mason added.

Something his parents definitely didn't seem to have.

"I suppose you could try it," his mother said slowly. "Is Brody willing to try it with you?"

Mason wasn't going to give her the satisfaction of knowing that Brody was the one who had talked him into it.

"I think so," he said. He reached down to rub Dog's silky head. Dog didn't seem to find it strange that Mason was going to play a sport. "I mean, yeah, he is."

His mother looked somewhat relieved.

But then: "Basketball," she said in bewilderment.

"Basketball," his dad echoed, gazing down at his puzzle. "Wait—it's an eight." He wrote 8 down in the square where he had just erased 9.

"I think we need to sign up for it today," Mason said. For good measure, he added with false heartiness, "Believe me, this is going to be great!"

His parents stared at each other in silent disbelief.

Mason's parents drove Mason and Brody to the county YMCA that afternoon to drop off their registration forms for the six-game late-fall basketball season.

"I know we could do it online," Mason's mother said. "But if everybody does everything online, there won't be any jobs left for actual human beings."

The actual human being sitting at the information desk at the Y was a teenage boy who was chewing gum. Mason knew his mother disapproved of gum chewing in public, so he wondered if she was sorry that she had chosen to support a job for this particular actual human being.

"Now, the boys will be on the same fourth-grade team, won't they?" she asked. Mason's dad had already placed the registration forms on the desk and looked ready to go.

"If you put that on the form," the boy said. He wore a name tag that gave his name as Jonah.

"We did. And do you know who their coach will be? They've never played basketball before." She lowered her voice, but Mason could still hear her perfectly: "This is my son's first experience with a team sport, so I want to make sure he gets a coach who is, you know, positive. And encouraging."

Jonah shrugged and shifted his gum from one cheek to the other. "Usually one of the parents does it. Or sometimes a guy who likes coaching."

"But do the coaches have experience?" Mason's mom pursued. "Or training of some kind?" She shot Mason's father a worried look.

Jonah shrugged again. Mason could tell that his mother thought that this actual human being was a disappointment.

As they turned onto Mason's street on the way home, Mason saw a small moving van parked in front of the house next door—not in front of Brody's house, which was next door to Mason's house on one side, but in front of the other house, next door on the other side.

"I wonder if Mr. Taylor is moving," Mason's mother said. "He didn't mention anything to us about it, and I haven't seen a for-sale sign."

Mason knew Mr. Taylor only as a middle-aged, rather stout, balding man who came outside occasionally to mow his lawn or take in the newspaper.

"Maybe somebody's moving in who has a kid our age!" Brody sounded excited.

Mason didn't say anything, but he didn't want any new kids on their street. Brody had lots of other friends, and Mason had other friends, too, mainly a girl at school named Nora. But it would make things complicated to have another kid right next door, coming over whenever he and Brody were outside with Dog, wanting to take part in all their games.

Mr. Taylor appeared in his yard.

"Are you moving, Jerry?" Mason's mother called over to him.

"No," he called back. "My mother is coming to live with me. We're moving in some of her furniture so she'll feel more at home."

As Mason's dad opened the door of their house, Dog came bounding out to greet them, trying to lick both Mason's and Brody's faces at the same time, while barking his welcoming bark and wagging his welcoming tail.

Mr. Taylor came up the front walk and said something to Mason's father that Mason couldn't hear.

"Oh, we understand completely!" Mason's dad said. "I'll speak to the boys about it. I'm sure it won't be a problem."

Speak to the boys about what?

When Mr. Taylor had gone back to his yard to supervise the movers, Mason's dad said to Mason and Brody, "Mr. Taylor said his mother—Mrs. Taylor—doesn't like dogs. So be sure to keep Dog under control when she's out in the yard, okay?"

"Sure," Brody said.

"Sure," Mason said.

He wasn't worried. He didn't particularly like *dogs* himself, just Dog. Nobody could not like Dog.

"Do you think our team is going to have a name?" Brody asked as the two boys sprawled out on the floor of Mason's family room, with Dog sandwiched between them. "We could call ourselves the Fighting Bulldogs. Do you think that's a good name?"

"Maybe," Mason said.

But Mason didn't like bulldogs: he only liked golden retrievers—one particular golden retriever. And he didn't like fighting dogs: Dog was completely sweet and friendly. And finally, Mason didn't think he was going to be much of a fighting bulldog himself.

This is going to be great! Brody had told Mason.

This is going to be great! Mason had told his parents.

Why did Mason have the feeling that it was going to be disastrous instead?

2

"Good morning, team!" Coach Joe greeted all the students in Mason's fourth-grade class on the Monday after Mason had signed his life away to the YMCA.

Coach Joe was not Mason's basketball coach. Coach Joe was Mason's fourth-grade teacher. That's what he wanted kids to call him: Coach Joe. Mason had been suspicious at first. Coach Joe loved sports—obviously!—and he talked about sports all the time. Mason suspected that Coach Joe thought it would be a tragedy to grow up without taking part in a team sport.

Still, as a teacher, Coach Joe was positive and encouraging—the very qualities Mason's mother had requested in a basketball coach for Mason. All the kids liked him.

"Come on up for our morning huddle," Coach Joe told the class.

Mason and Brody found places next to each other on the football-shaped rug by Coach Joe's stool, as they always did. Nora sat with them, too. Nora was also tall. In her case, it probably did mean that she'd be good at basketball. Mason didn't know if the fourth-grade teams were mixed boys and girls, or if boys and girls played in separate leagues.

There was a lot he didn't know about basketball.

And wasn't looking forward to finding out.

As usual, Mason and Brody had chosen a spot as far away as possible from Dunk Davis. Dunk was built like a football player, not a basketball player. Mason hoped that Dunk wouldn't be playing basketball at the Y, but Dunk played every sport known to man, plus a few of his own invention, such as "throw a basketball at Brody's head" and "throw a football at Mason's stomach." And a boy named Dunk might well go out for a sport that involved dunking.

"All right, team," Coach Joe said, once everybody had settled down. "We're starting a new unit in social studies this week, a brand-new ball game. Now that we've studied Native Americans and the age of exploration, we're going to move into the colonial period. And for language arts, we'll focus on factual writing, with each of you writing a report on a famous figure of the American Revolution."

Nora's face brightened. Mason knew that Nora loved facts.

"We're going to be learning about everyday life in the thirteen colonies: what folks wore, what they ate, what they did for fun. And we'll have Colonial School Day and run our class the way they would have done it in 1750."

He paused for effect, his eyes twinkling with anticipation of what he was going to say next.

"You'll have to call me Master Joseph, and naughty boys and girls will wear a dunce cap and sit on a stool in the corner."

Mason couldn't tell if Coach Joe was joking or not. He was pretty sure he'd be safe from the dunce cap. But in 1750, Dunk would have been sitting on that stool in the corner all day long.

"All right, team," Coach Joe dismissed them. "Back to your desks, and we'll rewind a few centuries and see what we find."

* * *

Most days Mason and Brody walked home from school together. Today, as they passed Mr. Taylor's house, Mason saw a small sign placed on the edge of the lawn.

It said NO DOGS.

In case a dog couldn't read, the sign also had a black silhouette of a dog in a red circle with a red line drawn through it.

Maybe because of his name, the sign seemed to be directed specifically at Dog, like a sign saying NO MASONS or NO BRODYS, complete with a crossed-out caricature of their faces.

"She hasn't even *met* Dog yet!" Mason burst out. "He hasn't done anything to her!"

On Dog's walk yesterday evening, Mason had been careful to go in the opposite direction, so Dog hadn't so much as stepped on the *sidewalk* by the Taylors' house.

Even Brody looked troubled by the unfairness of this unprovoked ban on any and all dogs, however wonderful. But then he said, "Well, that explains it. She *thinks* she doesn't like dogs because she hasn't met *our* Dog."

Mason shook his head. "She's not going to change," he predicted darkly.

"You changed," Brody pointed out.

"That was different. Besides, I *did* like Dog from the start. I just didn't know it."

"Maybe she just doesn't know it."

Now Mason was getting angry. He was nothing like a crabby, nasty-tempered, dog-hating, witchy old lady.

"Maybe I'll put a sign on my yard. It'll say NO OLD

LADIES. And I'll put a picture of a cane in a red circle with a big red line through it."

Brody looked shocked. "Mason!"

"Okay, okay, I won't put the cane." His parents would never let him display a sign like that, anyway. His mother hated what she called stereotypes of people—prejudiced views of somebody based on their race or sex or age.

But didn't Mrs. Taylor have a stereotyped, prejudiced view of Dog based on his species?

From the corner of his eye, Mason saw some movement at one of the upper windows of the Taylor house.

"Don't look now," he told Brody in a low voice, "but somebody is spying on us."

"Mrs. Taylor?" Brody looked up, of course, even though Mason had just told him not to.

"Who else?" Mason muttered. "Come on, Brody, let's go home and see Dog. Our Dog of Greatness."

"Don't tell Dog about Mrs. Taylor, okay?" Brody said.

"Okay," Mason agreed.

But he had a feeling Dog would find out about Mrs. Taylor soon enough.

On Thursday morning at breakfast, as Mason was eating his plain Cheerios with milk, his mother said, "I got an email. There's a meeting at the Y tonight for all kids who are doing basketball, along with their parents."

"Do we have to go?" Mason asked.

"Of course!"

"Do you and I both have to go?" Mason's dad asked her.

"Along with their *parents*," she repeated, with emphasis on the s at the end of the word. "Honestly, Dan. Sometimes you're as bad as Mason!"

Then she stopped herself, as if remembering that you were supposed to avoid labeling your child—not to mention his father—in that way.

"It's going to be fun! We can find out if any of your other friends are on your team. And who your coach is going to be! Maybe they'll hand out your T-shirts."

Yes, and then she'd want Mason to put his on so she could take a picture of him to send to all the relatives: *See, Mason is doing a team sport at last!* And great would be the rejoicing throughout the land.

Then Mason remembered that he was supposedly the one who had wanted to sign up to do basketball, that doing basketball had supposedly been all his own idea.

"Oh, goody," Mason said.

On the way to school that morning, Mason and Brody passed the NO DOGS sign on the Taylors' lawn. So far Mason had resisted the temptation to let Dog pee on the Taylors' lawn. Mason scowled up at the upstairs window in case any dog-haters were spying again today.

That afternoon, after math time, one of the parent helpers—Emma Averill's mom—came to their class to help do a colonial craft with Coach Joe's class. Coach Joe had told them they'd be doing a different colonial craft every Thursday.

This week the craft was making pomander balls. Mason had never heard of pomander balls, but apparently they were wildly popular in the thirteen colonies.

To make a pomander ball, you took an orange, stuck it full of cloves, and rolled it in cinnamon.

"And then," Emma's mom said, "you can put it in your bureau drawer and all your unmentionables will smell so nice."

Mason guessed that "unmentionables" were underwear. He would have thought that people in the eighteenth century would have had enough problems—dying of diseases like yellow fever, getting ready to fight King George III for their liberty—without worrying about making their underwear smell nice.

It was hard forcing a clove into the thick rind of an orange. Already Mason's thumb was sore from trying.

"Use a toothpick to make a hole first," Emma's mom suggested, offering him one from the small box she had brought with her.

Mason stabbed his orange with a toothpick. The point of the toothpick broke off.

Across the room, Dunk seemed to have given up on cloves altogether and was juggling three oranges. The only problem was that Dunk didn't know how to juggle. All three oranges landed on the floor and rolled under other people's desks.

Luckily Coach Joe was in the room, making a pomander ball of his own. "Easy, Dunk," he said.

His juggling performance over, Dunk crawled on the floor to retrieve the fruit. Mason couldn't imagine that Dunk's pomander ball was going to be an appealing addition to anybody's underwear drawer.

Nora raised her hand. "How did people in colonial times get oranges?" she asked. "I mean, they couldn't

buy them at the grocery store. Or grow them, unless they lived in Florida. And Florida wasn't one of the thirteen colonies."

Emma's mom looked stumped. "Well, I don't know."

"They would have used apples," Coach Joe said. "Apples grew well in all of the thirteen colonies."

"Then why aren't we using apples?" Nora asked.

That was a good question. In addition to being more historically accurate, apples had softer skin, so it wouldn't take two years to insert each clove. The score on Mason's pomander ball now was orange 5, Mason 0.

"Most people use oranges or lemons nowadays," Emma's mom said. "Because they smell so refreshing— that wonderful citrus aroma. And oranges and lemons last longer."

Mason hadn't known that anybody made pomander balls nowadays. Concern for having nice-smelling underwear must span the centuries.

He looked over at Nora's pomander ball. Clever Nora had managed to insert her cloves in neat up-and-down lines that made her orange look sort of like a miniature basketball.

Brody was already rolling his pomander ball in cinnamon. The last step was to wrap it in a square of fabric and tie it with a red ribbon. Brody gave his finished pomander ball a loving little pat.

Mason tried to jam another toothpick into his. The toothpick broke off in his hand, of course.

Orange 6, Mason 0.

3

The basketball meeting was held at the Y, in a large gym at the end of a long hallway. Mason could tell by looking around that *all* basketball players and their families were not in attendance. Only a few families had bothered to come. Mason and his parents sat on the folding chairs next to Brody and his dad.

"The meeting is really for families new to the Y youth sports programs," Brody's dad explained, "or for teams that are just forming, like this one."

Mason didn't recognize any other kids he knew from school. Dunk wasn't there; maybe that meant Dunk wasn't doing basketball, or maybe it meant that he was on another team, or maybe his family just hadn't come to the meeting. Mason couldn't decide if it would be better to have Dunk on the same team or a different team. Was it better to have Dunk on your side, but see more of him, or have Dunk ready to bounce a basketball off your head, but only once in a while?

"Do you know who the coach will be?" Mason's mom asked Brody's dad.

"All I know is that it won't be me," Brody's dad said. "I'm already coaching Cammie's team."

"There's that kid again," Mason's mother said, nodding her head toward the door. "That Jonah person. Mr. Chewing Gum. I hope he's not the one running the meeting."

Sure enough, Jonah was slouching by the door, staring vacantly at no point in particular.

Then a middle-aged man entered the gym, clipboard in hand. Mason could see his mother's shoulders relaxing with relief.

"Welcome to YMCA youth basketball!" the man announced in a booming voice.

Mason mostly tuned out as the man talked about the values that team sports were going to instill in the kids this season. Perseverance. Always giving 110 percent. Striving for your personal best. Respect. Fairness. Team play. Sportsmanship.

Mason barely listened as the man talked about rules. The main rule, he gathered, was to wear shoes with the right kind of soles. He could handle that. His mother, he saw, was busy taking notes.

"Any questions?" the man asked.

She put up her hand. He could have guessed she'd be the first one with a hand in the air.

"Who is going to be the coach for the team?"

The man smiled. Something about the smile made Mason nervous.

"I'm glad you asked. YMCA teams are coached by volunteer coaches. Usually it's a parent on the team. Every once in a while we'll get a college kid who's willing to help us out in the coaching department. But we start by asking the parents. So that's the last thing we need to do this evening: identify a coach for this newest team."

No one spoke.

"It's a great way to be involved with your kid and his friends," the man said. "Coaching gives you a chance to relate to your son and be a part of his world in a whole new way."

Still no hands.

"Now, we hate to cancel a team. We hate to turn

away any kid who wants a chance to play. So, Jonah here, who helps us at the registration desk, is willing to fill the coaching slot if we can't find anyone else."

Jonah gave a small shrug of agreement.

From next to him, Mason heard his mother's sharp intake of breath. She whispered something to his dad. Mason knew she wasn't going to think this "Jonah person" was an acceptable, positive coach to make a lifelong athlete out of her son.

Then she raised her hand.

"Ma'am?"

"My husband will do it."

Mason whirled around to stare at his dad, who looked clearly bewildered at how he could have come to the meeting as an ordinary dad and left as the team's brand-new coach.

Brody clapped, and Brody's dad gave Mason's dad an appreciative whack on the back.

Mason didn't say anything until they were walking to the car in the chill autumn darkness.

"But, Dad, you don't know anything about coaching basketball."

"I know, son," his dad said. "Believe me, I know."

* * *

By Saturday morning, Mason's dad was looking more cheerful.

"How hard can it be?" he asked at breakfast, talking more to himself than to anybody else. Or maybe talking more to Dog, who was always a good listener. "This isn't the NBA. It isn't the NCAA. It isn't even high school. It's fourth-grade basketball."

"Did *you* ever play basketball?" Mason asked him.

"Not on a team. But we played in P.E. I'm sure we must have played in P.E. We did a little bit of everything in P.E., as I remember."

"What team sport *did* you play?"

His dad hesitated. "Well, sports weren't such a big thing back then as they are now."

"You didn't do a team sport. Mom!" Mason alerted his mother, who was flipping through a knitting magazine, looking for ideas to feature in the online knitting newsletter that she edited. "Dad didn't do a team sport, and he turned out okay."

His mother glanced up from her magazine. "Dan, I thought you played Little League Baseball. Didn't you tell me you played Little League?"

"I told you that my parents *wanted* me to play Little League. I stuck it out for a couple of practices,

33

then quit after the first game. The pitcher beaned me in the head with a ball—in all fairness to him, I think he was trying to get it over the plate but had a little problem with aim. So I developed sort of a—well, I wouldn't call it a phobia, exactly. Let's just say a fear. A fear of being hit in the head by another ball. So that ended my illustrious baseball career."

Mason's mother gave her husband a worried look.

"Basketball is different," his father said quickly. "People don't throw a basketball as hard, and you'll have your hands free to catch it before it hits you. Besides"—he added with a grin—"you're going to have a much better coach than I did."

Mason's mother started to say something. Then she turned her gaze back to her magazine. Mason could see the picture she was studying—some sort of shapeless poncho with loud, zigzaggy green and pink stripes that made the kid wearing it look like—no, there was nothing that could be compared to how that kid looked wearing it.

A sudden new suspicion burst upon him.

"Mom, did *you* ever do a team sport?"

The split second of silence before she answered

was all Mason needed to know that he had guessed correctly.

As if sensing something new in the conversation, Dog whacked his tail against Mason's leg; Mason reached down and rubbed Dog's favorite spot behind his ears.

"But, Mason." His mother recovered quickly. "We're so proud of *you* for wanting to try a team sport. When you don't like trying anything new. And for wanting to try basketball, of all things. When basketball is such a challenging sport, and when—"

"Look," Mason's dad interrupted. "I ordered a book last night online, all about how to coach basketball, specifically geared for parents who have never coached before. Tracy, this is going to make all the difference."

Mason's mother still looked worried.

"I put a rush on it, so it should be here Monday afternoon, in time for our first practice Tuesday evening. This book is going to tell me everything I need to know about coaching, and we're going to have a great basketball season!"

Or not.

But Mason gave his dad a sickly grin.

After breakfast, Brody came over so that he and Mason could throw balls for Dog in the new-fallen snow. It had snowed a couple of inches the night before—the first snow of the season usually came by Halloween in Colorado—and the yard was a sparkling expanse of white in the morning sun.

Mason and Brody tried to play fetch with Dog whatever the weather. If Dog didn't get enough of an opportunity to carry balls and sticks in his mouth, he tended to use his mouth to start chewing things he wasn't supposed to chew. Like Mason's mother's knitted pillows. Or—once—the elementary school's stuffed-dragon mascot, which had come home to be repaired and had been demolished by Dog instead.

Dog excelled at catching tennis balls even in the snow. Sometimes he leaped into the air on his three legs and caught the ball in his mouth. Someone should invent a team sport for dogs. Mason and Brody could coach it together, and Dog would be the star of the team.

Pleased at this thought, Mason tossed his next ball higher into the air, sending it soaring over Dog's head onto the snowy lawn of the house next door.

The Taylors' house. The ball landed right next to the NO DOGS sign.

In a flash, Dog sprinted after it and brought it back to Mason, tail wagging with delight at another mission accomplished. A trail of footprints followed behind him across the Taylors' previously unmarred blanket of snow.

Mason looked up at the Taylors' upstairs window. Sure enough, the curtain was pulled back, and he saw a glimpse of someone's face.

Maybe Mason's sign should say NO SPIES, with a bright red line through a picture of a pirate spyglass.

"Do you think she saw him?" Brody asked.

"Uh-huh."

They threw a few more balls for Dog, but the fun had gone out of the game. Dog seemed to sense it, too. He started chasing a squirrel that scampered up a tree to escape him. Not that Dog would ever hurt a squirrel. Dog was the best dog in the world and would never hurt anything.

"Let's go in," Mason said.

Then they saw Mr. Taylor coming up the front walkway to Mason's house. Ever friendly, Dog dashed over to greet him.

"Beautiful morning," Mr. Taylor said heartily, stooping down to give Dog an awkward pat.

Mason knew Mr. Taylor hadn't come out of his house to comment on the weather, speaking the only two words he had ever spoken thus far to Mason.

The boys nodded. Dog wagged his tail.

"Sure is," Brody added.

"I just wanted to say—to ask you—if you'd make an effort to keep your dog—I'm afraid I don't know his name—"

"Dog," Mason said.

Mr. Taylor looked baffled, as people often did when Mason told them Dog's name.

"To keep your dog in your yard. My mother is particular about things—like how the snow looks when it's all fresh and new—"

Mr. Taylor gestured toward Mason's well-trampled yard, where the snow was stamped down into dirty slush.

"And I think I mentioned the other day that she doesn't—"

"Like dogs," Mason finished the sentence for him wearily.

"That's right." Mr. Taylor sounded apologetic.

Mason decided against making any witty remark like, *What a coincidence! Dog doesn't like old ladies!*

"Sure," Brody said.

"Sure," Mason echoed.

With Dog trailing behind them, they trudged back inside.

4

Coach Joe's class went to the library on Monday to find books for their Famous Figures of the American Revolution reports, the big language-arts project for the trimester.

Nora was looking discouraged. "I wanted to do a famous woman of the American Revolution, but all the ones I looked up on the computer at home aren't real."

"What do you mean, aren't real?" Brody asked.

The three of them had grabbed some books from the selection the librarian had prepared on a cart and were looking at them together in the reading nook over by the windows.

"Like Betsy Ross. The thing I read about her said she didn't really make the first flag. Or Molly Pitcher.

She didn't really carry a pitcher of water to the wounded soldiers on the battlefield. I don't think she even existed."

"What about Martha Washington?" Mason asked. "She was real."

"She was just famous because she was married to someone famous."

"But maybe she helped him to become famous," Mason suggested. "She sent him off to war with extra-wonderful pomander balls so he had the nicest-smelling uniform in the whole army, and that's why they made him general."

Nora laughed. "Anyway, I decided to do Benjamin Franklin instead, because he was a scientist as well as a politician, and I'm going to be a scientist."

"I was thinking of doing him, too," Brody said. "I saw his printing shop the summer before last when my parents took us to Philadelphia, and I have a hat like his that I can wear if Coach Joe has us dress up."

Brody loved dressing up.

Mason didn't.

Brody loved Halloween, which was coming up this weekend. This year Brody was going to cover himself with green and purple balloons and be a bunch of grapes.

Mason hated Halloween. For the class party he was going to wear his regular clothes and say that he was a werewolf but it wasn't the full moon yet. He had been enormously relieved when he thought up that particular idea.

"Okay, I'll do Ben Franklin, too," Mason said. It might as well be unanimous.

"Is it okay if we all do the same person?" Brody asked.

"Sure," Nora said. "So long as we write our own reports. Coach Joe didn't say everybody had to do someone different."

After they each found a Ben Franklin book, they stood in line for checkout. Just ahead of them in line, Dunk was also carrying a book about Ben Franklin. Well, it wasn't as if Dunk could ruin Ben Franklin for everybody else just by writing a report about him.

Unlike the way Dunk could ruin basketball for everybody by being on their team. Or on a different team. Or on any team at all.

Mason might as well find out the worst. "Hey, Dunk, are you playing basketball this season?"

"Yeah, why?" Then Dunk seemed to answer his own question. "Don't tell me you guys are playing basketball. Brody the Midget? And Mason the Klutz?"

Mason didn't point out that he wasn't the one who had tried to juggle pomander-ball oranges and failed miserably. He couldn't remember ever having done a klutzy thing in front of Dunk. Except for that

time he had fallen over during the kindergarten concert while pretending to be a teapot short and stout.
But that didn't have anything to do with sports.

"Wait till you guys play my team," Dunk chortled.
"Do you know what the name of our team is?"

How could Mason possibly know the name of
Dunk's team when he hadn't even known for sure
that Dunk was *on* a team?

"The Killer Whales," Dunk told him.

"I never heard of any whales that were especially

good at basketball," Mason couldn't resist saying. Fighting bulldogs had to be better at basketball than killer whales. At least they had feet and lived on land.

"That's because you haven't heard of these whales," Dunk retorted. "But you will."

He whacked Mason in the shoulder with his Ben Franklin book in a way that wasn't very beneficial either for the book or for Mason's shoulder.

"You will," Dunk repeated.

On Tuesday night, Mason and his dad arrived at the first basketball practice twenty minutes early. The team practices were held not at the Y but at the elementary school. Mason's dad was clutching his coaching book, which had indeed arrived yesterday as promised. Already the book bristled with sticky notes marking the most important pages.

"The book said I need to figure out my coaching philosophy," Mason's dad said. "I need to decide the most important thing I want my players to learn."

"How to get the ball through the hoop?" Mason thought that was a good one, for starters.

"Not things like that. What *values* do I want you to learn?"

"Perseverance. Giving 110 percent. Striving for our personal best. Sportsmanship. Teamwork." Mason rattled them off. He must have been paying more attention the other night than he had realized.

"But which of those values is the *most* important? Do you want to know what I've decided? Which one I've picked as the core of my coaching philosophy? Sportsmanship. 'It's not whether you win or lose, but how you play the game.'"

That was probably a good choice, given that Mason was expecting their team to lose every single game.

"We may not be the winningest team," Mason's dad said.

An understatement, if Mason had ever heard one.

"But we can excel in sportsmanship. Unless—do you think I should have picked teamwork?"

"Sportsmanship is good," Mason reassured him. He was confident that just about any team could beat the Killer Whales on sportsmanship. "But aren't we also going to have to learn stuff like how to actually play the game?"

"Of course. Tonight we're going to work on"—he checked his notes—"layups. And dribbling. And different kinds of passes. But I'm hoping most of the kids will already have some of those basics down from P.E." His brow furrowed with worry. "We're not going to have to start from scratch, are we?"

Mason felt sorry enough for his dad that he said, "Nah. We did a lot of that stuff in P.E."

For three weeks.

Almost a year ago.

Toward seven o'clock, the rest of the team began trickling in. Brody was first, of course, followed by Jeremy, also from Coach Joe's class, and three boys Mason didn't know from the neighboring town. Was that going to be the whole team? Six kids, all of whom had probably never played team basketball before or they'd be on a team already?

Mason thought his dad did a good job of welcoming everybody and making his speech about the importance of sportsmanship. He didn't talk too long, and he said the positive, encouraging things Mason's mom had wanted from a coach for Mason.

"I know each one of you has a unique contribution to make to this team," he concluded. "And I'm here to help you make that contribution."

Mason wondered what his own unique contribution

was going to be, or if he even had a unique contribution. He suspected that his father might have taken that line directly from his coaching book. Still, it was a positive, encouraging line.

"Okay, team!" Now his dad sounded like Coach Joe. In fact, perhaps inspired by Coach Joe, he had asked the kids to call him Coach Dan. "Coach Dan" and "Coach Dad" sounded enough the same that if Mason called him Coach Dad, no one would be likely to notice.

They started with some stretches to warm up their muscles, and then did a dribbling drill back and forth across the gym. One chubby, red-haired kid, Dylan, kept losing control of his basketball and having to chase it across the gym. Then Mason was partners with Dylan for a passing drill. Dylan could neither catch a ball thrown to him nor throw a ball so that anybody else could catch it.

Maybe Dylan's unique contribution to the team was going to be making everyone else feel better about himself in comparison.

Mason's dad stepped in to offer Dylan some pointers. "Good job!" he praised, after Dylan finally caught the ball one time instead of throwing up his hands to shield his face.

Mason could only imagine what Dylan's parents had said to coax him into trying basketball. If he himself had been the coach, he would have suggested that Dylan reconsider this choice. But if Dylan quit the team, they would have just five players—the bare minimum for a team, without a single substitute.

In his opening remarks, Mason's dad had urged the players to try to find a friend or two to join. But Mason's second-best friend was Nora, and the fourth-grade teams weren't co-ed. And Brody's second-best friend, Sheng, was already on a team.

During the layup drill, Mason was gratified when a couple of his shots went through the basket. He wished his mother had been there to see that her son was more talented at basketball than she seemed to think.

"Water break!" Coach Dad announced.

Mason thought it might be a good idea to end the first practice a bit early—or a lot early—so that the players wouldn't get overtired and strain their muscles. A little bit of basketball practice went a long way, in Mason's opinion. But after the quick water break, his dad put the players back to work, practicing one-on-one offensive and defensive strategies.

This time Mason wasn't stuck with Dylan. Instead, he was paired with Brody, the king of hustle. Scrappy little Brody kept knocking the ball out of Mason's hands and diving after it. For a moment, Mason felt the tiniest flicker of dislike for Brody. Why would a *friend* try so hard to take the ball away from another friend?

"Mason, you're not trying," Brody complained after he made the next basket.

"Maybe you're trying too hard," Mason shot back.

"That's what hustle *is*," Brody explained, grabbing the ball away from Mason and aiming it at the hoop.

Mason was glad when Brody missed, but then, too busy smirking, he forgot to go for the rebound. Brody snagged it and shot it again; the ball went in this time.

"Twelve to two," Brody announced.

Oh, put a sock in it, Mason wanted to say.

Finally, practice was almost over.

"One more practice—one!—and then we have our first game!" Coach Dad told the team as they did their cool-down stretches. "Remember to try to find some friends to join us. We could really use a few more kids."

Brody walked home with Mason and his dad. Even after a solid hour of running and jumping, Brody kept springing into the air to shoot imaginary baskets, doubtless racking up an ever-higher imaginary score in his head.

"Cut it out, Brody," Mason said. "Practice is over."

"Brody has the right idea," his dad said. "Good job tonight, Brode. Oh, and good job, Mason," he added, clearly as an afterthought.

Surely his coaching book would say that a coach wasn't supposed to have favorites. Right now it seemed as if Mason's dad might have forgotten that particular piece of coaching advice.

5

On the second colonial-crafts Thursday in Coach Joe's class, the parent helper was Sheng's mom, Mrs. Lin, and the colonial craft was making corn-husk dolls.

It was too late in the year for anyone to be able to gather corn husks from a cornfield, so Sheng's mom had bought several big packages of corn husks from a Mexican food store. Selling corn husks at a food store seemed somewhat strange to Mason.

Even Mason's mom, who liked to cook all kinds of foods from other countries and cultures, had never yet tried to make Mason eat corn husks or anything wrapped in them.

Mason rolled his moistened corn husks into a little bundle and tied it with a piece of string, as Mrs. Lin had demonstrated. Then he flipped the husks over the tied string and tied them again to form the doll's head.

Brody was already talking to his doll.

"Now I'm going to make your *arms*," he told the doll. "I'm going to make you a nice pair of arms!"

The heads didn't have faces painted on them yet; the students couldn't draw on the faces until the dolls were all done and had time to dry, or their faces would smear. A smeary face was worse than no face at all. So Brody had to imagine the expression on his doll's face. He held her—him?—it?—up in front of him and made the doll give a little shake of joyful anticipation.

"My doll's head is too big," Mason complained. "I tied the string down too low."

"A big head is good!" Brody reassured him. "It means your doll will be extra smart because of all those extra brains."

Mason doubted that greatly.

Nora was working on her doll with quiet competence. Her doll's arms were already done, complete with hands, and she had tied its waist and fluffed out its long skirts.

"You don't have any other dolls, do you?" Mason asked her. He had been to Nora's house a few times and had never seen any dolls or stuffed toys in her room, just her ant farm.

"No. I mean, what's the point?"

Mason's thought, exactly.

"Are you going to make your doll a boy or a girl?" Brody asked Mason.

Mrs. Lin had told them they could either give their dolls a long full skirt or tie the corn husks at the bottom of the doll into two sections to form its legs.

Nora gave a little snort. "You mean, is your doll going to have pants or a dress? You aren't a boy just because you have on pants." She pointed to her own blue jeans. "Every single girl in our class is wearing pants, even Emma."

"But this is back then," Brody said. "In colonial times."

"I know. But even nowadays, restroom doors have a picture of a person in a dress, and that means women, or a picture of a person in pants, and that means men. Which is dumb."

"I'm going to make my doll a girl," Brody said. "She just seems like she's a girl."

Mason was going to make his a girl, too, to save the extra step of tying legs.

"I'm going to name you Abigail," Brody told his doll. "Do you like that name? Abigail?"

The doll gave another little happy shake.

"She likes it," Brody said.

Dunk had finished his doll. He walked over to Mason's desk with it. Dunk's doll—if you could call it that—was the worst-looking corn-husk doll Mason had ever seen. No one could have guessed that this bunch of corn husks tied in random places was a corn-husk doll if it hadn't been made during a class on how to make corn-husk dolls.

Dunk made his corn-husk doll leap into the air and then jerked it forward.

"Two!" Dunk shouted.

Mason figured out that Dunk's doll had just made a slam dunk, scoring two points for the Killer Whales.

In the effort, though, one of the corn husks slipped from its string and dropped onto Mason's desk.

"Your doll is falling apart," Mason pointed out politely.

"Yeah, well, after our first game, your team is going to be falling apart."

Another corn husk came loose as Dunk waved his doll in Mason's face.

"Actually, your doll just *fell* apart," Mason said.

Mason was pretty good with snappy lines.

But it would take a lot more than snappy lines to beat the Killer Whales in basketball.

The snow had long melted by the weekend, so when Mason and Brody were outside on Saturday afternoon playing catch with Dog, no telltale footprints betrayed Dog for having run twice into the Taylors' yard, chasing his ball. Besides, surely Mrs. Taylor didn't sit peering out her window every single minute of the day just in case a dog crossed over her property line.

Brody's next throw went wild, and this time Dog did dart all the way to the Taylors' front walk to retrieve it. But Mason couldn't get too stressed about it. Dog wasn't peeing or pooping in the Taylors' yard, he wasn't making any noise except for one or two friendly barks that couldn't bother anybody, and he had never bitten anyone, ever. Well, except for chewing up Puff the Plainfield Dragon.

How could anybody not like Dog? Or mind the sight of him out playing on a sunny autumn afternoon?

Then, a few minutes later—to Mason's utter disbelief—a panel van with CITY OF PLAINFIELD ANIMAL CONTROL written on the side pulled up in front of his yard. A man in a green uniform got out of the van, carrying a clipboard.

"Hey, kids," the man said. "Whose dog is this?"

"Mine," Mason and Brody answered together. Dog belonged to both of them equally, and they both loved him equally, and if someone was going to get in trouble because of Dog, they would both get in trouble equally.

"Are your folks around?" the man asked.

Before Mason could stammer out an answer, his dad was there, coming down the front walk.

"Hi, I'm Dan Dixon," he introduced himself. "Is there a problem?"

"One of your neighbors called us about an off-leash dog running wild," the animal-control man explained. "Said it was this fellow here."

"But surely you can have a dog off leash in your own yard," Mason's dad said.

"That's right. But only in your own yard."

"He wasn't running wild!" Mason burst out.

"Dog would never run wild," Brody chimed in.

"We were just playing fetch—"

"And one time—well, a couple of times—"

"The ball went over to her yard, and Dog ran to get it, and he was in her yard for a total of—"

"Two seconds!"

"The boys are telling the truth," Mason's dad said. "They're very careful when they walk Dog, and they always clean up after him."

The animal-control man shook his head in an embarrassed way. "Look. I'm not going to give you a ticket for an off-leash violation. Frankly, well, the complaint strikes me as unreasonable. But I have to inform you that it will be on your dog's record now that there has been a complaint. So, boys, keep your dog out of the neighbor's yard, okay? Just keep him out of her yard."

He gave the four of them a friendly smile and even reached down and rubbed Dog's head the proper way behind his long, silky ears.

"Did you hear that, boys?" Mason's dad asked.

Both boys nodded.

Then the man gave another good-natured grin, climbed back into his van, and drove away.

"I *am* going to get that NO OLD LADIES sign," Mason muttered, once his dad had gone back into the house.

"But, Mason, she never comes out of her house, anyway."

Brody was right. Mason had never seen any sign of Mrs. Taylor, except for that telltale movement of the curtain in the upstairs window.

"So what are we going to do?" Mason asked.

"I don't know," Brody said. "Keep Dog out of her yard, I guess. But tonight, when I go trick-or-treating with Sheng and Julio, I'm not going to go to her house."

Mason wasn't going to go trick-or-treating at all. His costume was too hard to explain. So he was going to stay at home and help hand out candy to people who didn't mind wearing costumes.

Mason gave Dog a huge hug, hoping that Mrs. Taylor was looking out of her window now to see what true love looked like, something a mean old, nasty old dog hater could never know.

At basketball practice on Tuesday night—the last practice before the first game of the season, to be played on Saturday morning at ten—Mason's dad handed out the schedule for all the games, six of them. On the schedule the teams were identified by coach and number, and not by name. There were six teams total for fourth-grade boys; Mason was on team number five. He had no idea which team was the Killer Whales.

What if Dunk's team was in a different league altogether? That would be extremely wonderful, but things that were extremely wonderful, in Mason's experience, tended to fall under the heading "too good to be true."

It was interesting that there was no category of things that were too bad to be true, at least not that Mason had ever heard of.

No new kids had joined the team. Mason's dad repeated his plea.

"Guys, we really need three or four more players!"

Mason wondered if what his dad really meant was "three or four players who can actually play."

During the dribbling drill, Dylan's ball was as hopelessly out of control as the previous week, and Dylan still couldn't throw, catch, shoot, or guard. Dylan didn't have much hustle, either, though if you played as badly as Dylan, there was a lot to be said for keeping a low profile.

For the second half of the practice, Coach Dad split the boys into two teams to play three-on-three. Mason had Dylan on his team—of course—and a boy named Kevin. Brody's team had Matt and Jeremy. Jeremy was probably, all around, the best player on the team. Coach Dad's division of the players didn't seem very fair to Mason.

"So that we can tell the teams apart," Coach Dad said, "one team will be the Shirts and the other will be the Skins. Brody, your team will be the Shirts. Mason, your team will be the Skins."

Skins?

Kevin caught on more quickly and pulled his

T-shirt up over his head, leaving his bare chest exposed. Dylan copied him. Mason had to do the same, but it made him feel strange. It was one thing to take off your shirt in the summertime, running through the sprinkler with Dog and Brody. It was another thing to take off your shirt in front of people who might think your chest looked funny: too fat, too flabby, too skinny, too scrawny, too white. Dylan's chest, for example, definitely looked too fat, too flabby, *and* too white.

Mason liked the comfort of nice, plain, solid-colored T-shirts—blue, green, yellow, red—with no words or pictures on them. Every day Mason wore the same thing: a plain T-shirt, blue jeans in the winter or khaki shorts in the summer, brown socks. He cast a longing glance at his plain blue T-shirt, crumpled up on the floor in a miserable-looking ball. He didn't know if he could make any baskets without it.

The practice game began.

Jeremy scored right away. Then the Skins got the ball.

"Get open, Mason, so Kevin can pass to you!" Coach Dad called.

Mason tried, but dogged little Brody stayed on him.

Kevin passed to Dylan instead. Bad mistake. When Dylan dropped the ball, Matt dove for it and passed it to Jeremy, who took the shot. The ball teetered on the rim but didn't go in.

"Rebound!" Coach Dad shouted. "Mason, rebound! Good job, Brody!"

Brody leaped for the rebound, got it, shot again, and scored.

"Good job, Brody!"

That was how the rest of the game seemed to Mason. Either his dad was shouting, "Get open, Mason!" or "Mason, get on your man!" or "Mason, rebound!" or else he was shouting, "Good job, Brody!" or "Way to go, Brody!" or "Great hustle, Brody!"

He shouted various things to Jeremy, Kevin, and Matt, but Mason barely noticed. There was no point in shouting anything to Dylan except for "Watch out!"

The score at the end of the game was something like a million to four. Mason chose not to remember the exact numbers.

"Great practice, guys!" Coach Dad said as they had a water break before their final cool-down stretches.

"If you guys hustle like that on Saturday, we'll have a chance."

Well, Brody, Jeremy, Kevin, and Matt would have a chance. And even "a chance" hardly made victory sound very likely.

"But do try to rustle up a couple more players," Coach Dad pleaded. "We could really use some backups."

Maybe if they had enough other players, players who really wanted to play, Mason could quit. His dad had quit Little League, after all. Maybe quitting a sport ran in the male half of the Dixon family.

If only Mason didn't have to pretend to his parents that he wanted to play basketball—that he did like trying new things, after all. If only he didn't have to pretend that playing basketball was fun.

6

"Would you like me to fix you some scrambled eggs?" Mason's mother asked him on Saturday morning.

Mason stared at the person who was asking him such a preposterous question. The person looked like his mother and sounded like his mother and had the familiar anxious smile of his mother. But she was uttering words that no one who knew Mason—such as his own mother—could possibly say.

For reply, he stalked over to the pantry cupboard and pulled out his box of plain Cheerios. From the fridge he took the gallon jug of milk. Then he poured some Cheerios into a bowl and poured some milk onto the Cheerios.

"Some protein?" she persisted. "Wouldn't that be a good idea, before your first game?"

Mason started spooning Cheerios into his mouth.

His father staggered into the kitchen, bleary-eyed, hair not yet combed. He was carrying the coaching book, with one finger inserted into the chapter he had been reading—presumably the chapter on how to coach your team's first game. Mason hoped the chapter offered some discussion of what to do when your team had only six players, none of whom were any good at basketball, and one of whom was the worst player in the history of the game.

This time Mason's mother didn't venture any dietary suggestions. She poured her husband a cup of black coffee and set it in front of him on the table.

"What does the book say about getting ready for a game?" Mason asked.

"Well, some of it doesn't apply," his dad said. "I mean, doesn't apply to us."

Now Mason was truly curious. "Like what?"

"It says to bench your players if they come late, or act inappropriately during a game, even if they're your star players."

"We don't have any star players," Mason said.

"We have hardly any extra players, period."

"What else does it say?"

"I'm not supposed to yell at the referee if I disagree with a call. But I wouldn't do that, anyway. I'm not a yelling kind of guy."

That was true.

"And it said"—even though Mason's dad kept his finger firmly in the book, he seemed to have it memorized—"to make it our goal to win with grace or lose with dignity."

Mason assumed their team would be focusing on dignity.

"I just hope . . ." His dad finally pulled his finger out of the book and set it on the kitchen table so he could take a long sip of his coffee. "That poor kid Dylan. I hope he doesn't get so discouraged that he gives up on the game altogether."

Which would be a bad thing?

"And Brody—when a kid is so hopeful and enthusiastic all the time? It would be a shame if this first game took that away."

Mason waited for his father to go on to note all the ways today's crushing defeat would be devastating for Jeremy, Kevin, and Matt. Apparently devastating effects on his own son weren't such a huge source of worry.

"Now, Dan." Mason's mother had obviously had enough of her husband's mournful speech. "I think Mason's first game is going to be wonderful."

"You weren't at the practice," Mason told her.

"Well, what's that saying? The worse the dress rehearsal, the better the show. So the worse the practice, the better the game."

"Sports are"—his father began the sentence, but father and son finished it together—"different."

"Are you sure you don't want any scrambled eggs?" she asked Mason again. "Dan? Scrambled eggs?"

"No," father and son replied together.

Mason and his parents arrived at the Y while the previous game was still in play. Brody and his family—both his parents and his two older sisters, Cara and Cammie—showed up a few minutes later.

Gum-chewing Jonah was there, handing out team T-shirts to players as they arrived. The team color for team number five turned out to be yellow.

"I love yellow!" Brody sang out. "Yellow is my lucky color. What's your lucky color, Mason?"

"I don't have a lucky color," Mason told him.

As they waited at the edge of the gym, Mason

scanned the players out on the court—red shirts versus gray shirts—to see if one of the players was Dunk. He didn't recognize any large, lumbering, Dunklike object.

Then, from behind, someone whacked his yellow-shirted shoulder—hard. Mason didn't have to whirl around to identify the whacker.

Dunk was wearing a blue shirt, appropriate, Mason thought, for the Killer Whales. His nasty grin stretched from ear to ear.

"We're going to beat you, we're going to beat you," he chanted.

Dunk's coach apparently hadn't read the part of the coaching book about winning with grace, or had failed to mention that particular bit to his team.

"Does your team have a name?" Dunk asked.

They hadn't actually gotten around to voting on a name. The choice of a name, Mason thought, was the least of their problems.

"The Fighting Bulldogs," Brody said, going with the name he had put forward before.

Dunk laughed, as if that were a dumb name for a team, which it wasn't.

"We'll see how much fight you have left after our game," he sneered.

The previous game ended. The two teams filed past each other out on the court, shaking hands. Mason felt sorry for the losers having to shake hands with the winners.

If there was anything in the world he didn't want to do, it was to lose to Dunk and then shake his sweaty, pudgy hand.

After a few warm-up drills, Coach Dad summoned his players into a huddle.

"Team," Mason's dad said, "we are going to go out there and play with everything we've got. We're going to play our best. We're going to play to win. But there's one thing that's more important than winning. What's that?"

Sheer survival?

"It's how we play. If we win, we're going to win with grace. If we lose, we're going to lose with dignity."

Mason had to admit his dad made the lines sound great.

"Okay, team," Coach Dad said, "let's go play some basketball."

With six players on the team, five would be on the court to start, and only one would be on the bench to sub. If Mason had been the coach, he would have put Dylan on the bench, because Dylan was indisputably the worst player on the team. But the coaching book must have warned against making your worst player feel that he was the worst, even when it was obvious to everyone that he was the worst.

"Let's see," Coach Dad said, as if he were choosing the only nonstarter purely at random. "Mason, why don't you sit out for the first bit, and you'll rotate in as soon as we need you."

Did this mean that his dad thought that he, Mason, was the second-worst player on the team? Mason plopped himself down on the bench—actually, a folding chair—gloomily.

Until this moment, he would have thought the bench was the best place to be if you had to be on a basketball team at all. Why run around red-faced and sweaty, when you could relax restfully and watch it all as a detached, amused observer?

But it was hard to be a detached, amused observer when your team was getting slaughtered by Dunk's team. Player after player for the Killer Whales seemed to be dancing his way down the court, shooting, and scoring, practically as if the Fighting

Bulldogs weren't even there. It sure looked to Mason as if there was a lot of traveling going on.

Mason started watching the Whales' feet closely. At least twice he saw feet that seemed to be taking some extra steps. Why wasn't the ref calling a traveling violation?

Mason looked over at the ref. The ref was Jonah! Too busy chewing gum, presumably, to referee with any accuracy.

At the end of the first six-minute quarter, the score was 10–0.

Mason went in for Dylan, who looked stunned and would probably quit the team before the game was over. The Killer Whales had already rotated in their subs, so all their players were fresh as a daisy. One of the subs was Dunk. Mason felt a twinge of satisfaction that Dunk hadn't been a starter for the Killer Whales. Then he remembered that he himself hadn't been a starter for the Fighting Bulldogs, either.

Mason managed to get open enough that Jeremy passed to him. He took two dribbles down the court before a Killer Whale stole the ball. In the process, the Killer Whale whacked Mason's arm as well.

Mason gave a loud "Ow!" to alert the ref to the Whale's wrongful bodily contact. Hearing no whistle, he turned to glare at Jonah, who kept on calmly chewing his gum.

Mason sprinted after the fouling Whale and stole the ball back.

Fwee! The whistle sounded.

Was Jonah-the-ref kidding? Mason hadn't even touched the Whale, whereas the Whale had whacked Mason so hard his arm still stung.

Surely his dad would say something. A coach couldn't stand by and do nothing when a foul was unfairly called against one of his players. And when the player was his son! Could he?

Apparently he could. Too late, Mason remembered the coaching book's stupid commandment against yelling at the referee.

The Killer Whale took a free throw, when he deserved to be taken out of the game. The ball soared through the rim and net.

At the half, the score was 23–4.

Mason's dad got his sweaty, panting team into a huddle.

"Look," he said. "This is our first-ever game, played against a much more experienced team, with twice as many players. Given all that, I think we're doing pretty darn well."

"Besides, the ref is blind!" Mason burst out. A new idea popped into his brain, an idea that would explain everything. "I think the Killer Whales bribed him!"

They were buying Jonah's bubble gum!

"Now, Mason," his dad said.

"I didn't foul that kid. He fouled me!"

"In the heat of a play, it can be hard to see exactly who fouled whom," Coach Dad said mildly.

"But they kept traveling, too!"

"Well, sometimes the refs don't call every single violation for the first game in the season."

If Mason survived this basketball season—a big if—he was going to write his own coaching manual. It would have a chapter on how to protest an obviously corrupt and cheating referee.

And another on why you shouldn't treat your own son worse than everyone else on the team.

Even Brody looked subdued. "Well, it will all be over in twelve more minutes," he said, which was more the kind of thing Mason would say.

They lost, 43–8.

Then came the moment Mason was dreading above all others, the moment when the Killer Whales and the Fighting Bulldogs had to file past each other in the center of the court and shake hands.

Mason held out his hand the way everyone else was doing. But he made sure that the tips of his fingers never actually touched any Killer Whale fingers.

Dunk didn't dare say anything nasty with the two coaches standing right there. Mason knew Dunk would have plenty to say at school on Monday.

Win with grace? Ha! Lose with dignity? Ha!

Coach Dad should return that coaching book to the publisher and demand his money back.

7

Sunday afternoon, Mason and Dog went over to Nora's house. The day after the worst slaughter in the history of fourth-grade basketball was a good day for spending some peaceful, quiet time with a friend and her ant farm.

Until Mason had become friends with Nora, he had never heard of such a thing as an ant farm; he had never known anyone who had ants as pets. Though they weren't pets, really, for Nora. They were objects of scientific study. Nora did experiments on her ants—not experiments that could be fatal, but definitely experiments that might annoy an ant or two. She liked giving her ants a challenge and seeing what they would do.

Today she had placed her ant farm in the refrigerator.

"The refrigerator!" Mason was shocked. Still cold from walking the few blocks to Nora's house, he shivered on behalf of her poor refrigerated ants.

"Mason, if they lived in nature, as ants are supposed to live, they'd be outside all winter long."

Of course, Nora was right. But still.

She had rescued the ants from the fridge and placed their farm back in its usual spot on top of the bureau in her room.

"See how much more slowly they're moving," she commented.

Mason watched them going about their ant business. It looked like pointless motion, but Nora had told Mason that it was actually highly purposeful activity.

After their stint in the fridge, the ants did seem sluggish. This was one way that Dog was different from ants. Cold weather made him extra energetic and peppy. Mason reached down and rubbed Dog's ears.

"So how was your game yesterday?" Nora asked Mason.

"Horrible."

"You lost."

"Good guess."

"Not to Dunk's team?"

"Who else?"

Then Mason told Nora everything—how the Fighting Bulldogs had no subs; how bad Dylan stank; how bad they all stank, really; how the gum-chewing ref had been bribed to make bad calls by the corrupt and cheating Killer Whales.

Nora nodded thoughtfully for all of it until Mason mentioned the bribing of the ref.

"You don't know that," she said.

"The evidence points that way." Mason thought Nora would approve of an appeal to the evidence.

Nora shook her head. "Anybody can make a bad call."

"Especially if he's paid to make them."

"Oh, Mason."

Silently they watched the ants for a few more minutes.

"I wish I could quit," Mason said. "But then my mother would say, *Oh, you know how Mason is— Mason never likes doing new things.*"

"Well, you don't like doing new things."

"I still don't want to hear her say it."

"Anyway, I wouldn't quit just yet," Nora said.

"Why not?"

"I have a feeling things are going to get better for the Fighting Bulldogs."

Mason stared at her. Nora wasn't the kind of person who relied on feelings.

"You don't know that," he echoed her line to him from before.

Nora smiled. "Actually," she said, "I do."

"Forty-three to eight!" Dunk greeted Mason and Brody on the school playground the next morning.

"Wow, Dunk," Mason said. "I didn't know you could count that high."

"I knew your team would stink," Dunk continued. "I knew it would stink big-time. But forty-three to eight?"

Mason should have grabbed Brody's arm and walked away. Instead, he said, "Well, your team is just a bunch of no-good dirty cheaters."

"What are you talking about?"

"Traveling all the time. Fouling everybody. Bribing the ref."

"We did not!"

"Did, too!"

Brody wasn't saying anything. Mason knew Brody thought Mason was being a poor sport, but he wasn't. Besides, how could you lose with dignity if the other team wasn't even trying to win with grace?

The bell rang.

Mason and Dunk were still squabbling as they took their seats.

"Cheater!"

"Loser!"

Coach Joe appeared out of nowhere and laid a hand on each boy's shoulder. "What's going on, guys?"

"My basketball team beat Mason's team, and he's a sore loser," Dunk told Coach Joe.

"His team cheated! They bribed the ref!"

Coach Joe rubbed his chin. "That's a pretty serious accusation," he told Mason. "A very serious accusation, I'd say."

Mason knew Coach Joe meant that he shouldn't be accusing Dunk and his team of cheating unless he had real proof. Which he didn't have. Unlike the time Dunk had copied his football story for language arts and Nora had found the same story, virtually word for word, on the Internet. How could he prove that Dunk's team had cheated? It wasn't as if he could expect to see them handing Jonah huge bags full of chewing gum.

"For now," Coach Joe went on, "maybe we should just decide that what happens on the basketball court stays on the basketball court. What do you say?"

He gave both boys a friendly grin. But Mason couldn't stop seething.

In math that morning they did division. Mason wished he could divide Dunk into tiny pieces.

In science they learned about electricity. Mason didn't wish he could electrocute Dunk, but he wouldn't have minded giving him a small shock or two.

In P.E. they started their unit on basketball, the last thing that Mason needed more of in his life right now. But with all his practice in the last couple of weeks, he was definitely better at basketball than he had been last year.

As Mason had guessed, Nora was excellent at shooting, the best in the class. She looked directly at the basket, calm and collected, as if measuring the exact angle and distance she needed to shoot. In the ball would go.

For language arts, Coach Joe gave the class time to work on their reports. Mason read his library book about Ben Franklin and took notes on index cards.

Brody raised his hand. "Are we going to have a day when we dress up in colonial clothes?"

"On our Colonial School Day," Coach Joe answered, "you'll be encouraged but not required to wear period clothes, if you have any handy."

Brody's face lit up, presumably at the thought of himself in his three-cornered hat.

Mason felt his own face light up at the thought of Dunk in a dunce's cap.

And he and Nora could both wear their nice, normal, regular clothes, with no hats at all.

On Tuesday morning at breakfast, Mason's dad was still studying his coaching book. Mason hadn't seen him doing a sudoku puzzle since basketball season began. Maybe he had decided that coaching was challenging enough to stimulate his aging brain cells.

"Tonight we'll do pivot-shooting drills," his dad announced.

Mason swallowed a mouthful of plain Cheerios. He didn't know what pivot-shooting drills were, but he didn't need to know.

"Oh, and Mason, I got an email from the Y registration office, with some great news for our team."

Had Dylan decided to drop out?

"Four new kids are joining us. Four! It's going to make a world of difference, believe you me."

Mason didn't ask if his dad knew the names of the new players. He'd find out soon enough.

That night at practice, Mason and his dad were there first, as usual; this time Brody walked over to the school with them.

The others trickled in: Jeremy, Kevin, Matt, Dylan. Nobody else. Maybe the four new players had heard about last weekend's hideous defeat and changed their minds about joining.

Then the four new players came bounding into the gym. One was wearing a pink princess T-shirt. Another's long ponytail bobbed behind her as she ran across the court. The third had her hair held back from her face with sparkly clips.

The fourth was Nora.

8

"But—" Mason could hardly grasp the fact that Nora and three other girls were apparently now team members of the Fighting Bulldogs. "But fourth-grade YMCA teams aren't co-ed!"

"True," Nora said.

"So—?"

"There are boys' teams and girls' teams. Boys can't be on girls' teams, but girls can be on boys' teams."

Mason shook his head. "That doesn't make any sense."

"They think it does. They think the boys are going to be better than the girls, so it would be unfair to the girls to *make* them play against boys, but not to *let* them play against boys."

Mason lowered his voice so the rest of his team

wouldn't hear. "The boys on our team aren't better than *anyone*."

Nora laughed. "Anyway, Amy, Elise, Tamara, and I were all on a team last year, but this year half the team moved away or couldn't play, so we were just going to take a break from basketball. But then I made my plan."

If Mason had been a hugging kind of person, and if Nora had been a hugging kind of person, he would have hugged her.

Brody was already warming up by shooting some layups with Jeremy. The other three new players were shooting from outside, making a higher percentage of shots than anyone thus far in the short, doomed history of the Fighting Bulldogs.

Mason's dad was too excited about the new recruits to remember to do the warm-up stretches the coaching book had recommended. He skipped the pivot-shooting drill he had planned as well. Instead, after the usual shooting and passing drills, he put the players into one three-on-three game and one two-on-two game. This time Mason and Brody were on the same team, playing against Dylan and Nora.

Handicapped by Dylan, Nora couldn't overcome

the Mason-Brody duo, despite her shooting prowess. Mason appreciated Brody's hustle more when they weren't playing one-on-one against each other. It even proved to be catching. Mason leaped for the rebound of one of Nora's shots as if it really mattered who caught it.

Right then, ahead of Nora and Dylan 8–6, it did.

"Great game," Nora said as they stood in line at the water fountain for the water break.

"Thanks," Mason said, wiping his sweaty face with the bottom of his T-shirt: gross, but effective. This might be the first time in his life that he had ever won anything.

He hoped Nora knew he wasn't just thanking her for what she had said. He was thanking her for what she had done.

Thursday's colonial craft was punched-tin lanterns. The parent helper for the day was Mason's mom. She was good at all crafts, though knitting and sewing were her specialties. She had made a Puff the Plainfield Dragon costume for the first concert of the Plainfield Platters a few weeks ago. Brody had worn it to sing a solo of the school song. Still, it was strange having her there in the classroom, showing everybody how to make punched-tin lanterns.

Each student was given a tin can that had been filled with water and frozen solid. Mason's mother had prepared the cans yesterday and stored them in the freezer in the teachers' lounge. Mason and Brody helped her carry them to Coach Joe's classroom, using lids from large cardboard cartons as trays.

The cans were all different sizes.

"I want to make a tiny lantern." Brody pointed at the smallest can. "Or maybe a huge lantern! How many can we make?" he asked Mason's mother as they walked down the hall together.

"Just one, I'm afraid. It was hard enough coming up with twenty-five cans, believe me."

"Okay, I'll do the littlest one. Which can do you want, Mason?" Brody studied the cans intently, his head tilted to one side.

"Um—they're all fine," Mason said. They were all . . . cans.

Back in Coach Joe's room, Mason's mom showed everyone how to draw a design on the outside of the can with washable marker, and then how to hammer in holes with a big nail along the lines drawn. There were only six hammers—Mason didn't know where she had even found those six—so kids had to take turns. He also wondered what the point of the ice was supposed to be.

Nora raised her hand. "Why are they filled with ice?"

"It's easier to hammer the nails against some kind

of surface," Mason's mom said. "It gives you more control."

"But—where would colonial people have gotten ice? They didn't have freezers." Nora's face furrowed with another question. "And where would they have gotten cans?"

"They would have used flat sheets of tin, hammering them on a wooden table. Then they bent them into a lantern shape."

"Where did they get the tin?"

Now Mason's mother looked perplexed. Sooner or later, Nora always came up with a question the parent helpers couldn't handle.

Even Coach Joe seemed stumped by this one. He looked up from helping a student to reply. "I believe they imported it from England," he told Nora.

"But where did *they* get it? Are there tin mines, like coal mines? I never heard of tin mines. And if there were tin mines in England, why weren't there tin mines in America?"

"Those are good questions we can try to answer during library time," Coach Joe said. "But now we want to finish our punched-tin lanterns before the ice melts."

Before the ice melts even more. Mason's lantern was

already leaking melted ice water onto his desk. Luckily his mother had brought in towels for everyone to place under their cans. She had really thought of everything. Mason was impressed. It wasn't as if she supervised the making of twenty-five punched-tin lanterns every day.

A howl went up from across the room. It was Dunk.

"My finger! I hammered my finger!"

Maybe Mason's mother hadn't thought of everything. She hadn't thought of Dunk hammering his own finger instead of hammering his can. At least he had hammered his *own* finger; usually it was the person sitting next to Dunk who ended up injured.

Dunk was bawling as if he were two years old instead of almost ten.

"Oh, Dunk, let me see." Mason's mom examined Dunk's finger. "I think it'll be all right. Put your finger in the ice, inside your can, and go down to the health room, so they can take a look at it," she suggested, exchanging glances with Coach Joe, who nodded his approval.

Sniffling now, Dunk left the room, sucking his

wounded finger much more like a big baby than like a Killer Whale.

"I'm going to hang my lantern on my Christmas tree," Brody told Mason. "Along with my pomander ball and my corn-husk doll. But I won't light a candle in it so the tree won't catch on fire and burn the house down."

Good idea.

"What are you going to do with yours?" Brody asked Mason.

Mason's design on his can was just the letter M: M for "Mason."

"Is M for 'Mom'? Are you going to give it to your mom for Christmas?"

Another good idea.

"Uh-huh," Mason said.

Maybe his dad would like a lovely pomander ball for his underwear drawer.

And maybe Dog would like a nice, chewable corn-husk doll.

"Now that we have ten players, will you still put Dylan in to play?" Mason asked his dad as he and his parents were driving to the Y Saturday morning for their second game of the season.

Mason knew what his dad was going to say before he said it.

"Of course! Mason—"

"The coaching book says—"

"No! I don't need to read a coaching book to know that every kid gets a chance to play. I'd rather lose every single game all season long than not give all kids an equal chance to play."

Mason had a feeling his dad was going to get his wish.

The team they were playing today—green shirts—had two of Brody's other friends on it: Sheng and Julio. Brody ran over to greet them when he arrived in the gym a few minutes after Mason.

Mason scowled in Brody's direction. There was no need to be so chummy with the enemy team.

Coach Dad put Mason in to start this time, along with Jeremy, Kevin, Nora, and Elise.

Mason passed to Nora every chance he got. He always felt better when the ball was in Nora's capable hands. One time he passed to Nora even when Elise and Jeremy were in a better position to shoot.

Sheng was guarding Nora; he stole the ball, took it down the court, shot, and scored.

Mason thought of all the reasons he had never really liked Sheng.

"Mason, look to see who's open!" his dad called to him.

Mason still thought Nora not-open was a better bet than anybody else open.

The next time he tried to pass to Nora, Sheng leaped for the ball again. Mason was sure he saw Sheng's shoulder bump against Nora's, but the ref didn't call a foul; it was a different ref this time, not Jonah.

Sheng scored again.

Mason thought of all the reasons he positively disliked Sheng.

Even with Mason's turnovers, the score was tied 12–12 at the half. Four of the Fighting Bulldogs' baskets were Nora's; one was Jeremy's, one Elise's.

Mason hoped he would have at least one in-game basket to his credit before the season—and his illustrious basketball career?—was over forever.

At the halftime huddle, Coach Dad told the team to be sure to look to see who was open before passing to anybody. He didn't name any names, but Mason was sure everybody knew who he was talking about.

Brody played the second half; unfortunately, so did Dylan. Mason watched from the bench as Dylan managed to keep out of the way most of the time. Mason didn't see anybody passing to him, which was for the best. The ref didn't make any other bad calls that Mason noticed. Brody scored twice; Amy and Elise each scored once.

With twelve seconds left, the score was still tied: 20–20. The Y didn't allow fourth-grade games to go into overtime, so if no one scored in the next twelve seconds, the game would be recorded as a tie.

The ball went out of bounds. Brody took the ball for the in-bounds pass. From the bench, Mason saw him scan the court, looking for an open player.

The only person open was Dylan. The other team seemed to have given up on guarding him, apparently viewing him as a random kid in a yellow T-shirt who had wandered aimlessly out onto the court but wasn't really part of the game.

Brody passed to Dylan.

The ball bounced off Dylan's chest. He grabbed it and made the worst shot in the history of basketball.

The ball went straight up, two pathetic feet, nowhere near the basket, proving that there was no need for a green-shirted player to waste any time guarding Dylan.

Julio was on the ball in a flash, hurling it toward another kid who was in position to score.

Fwee! The ref blew his whistle to signal the end of the game. The Fighting Bulldogs had lost 22–20.

Because of Dylan.

No. Because of *Brody*.

9

"Terrific game, team!" Coach Dad said, after the team handshake, during which Mason was once again able to avoid any actual finger-to-finger contact with the other players.

Terrific game? Had his father failed to notice that the Fighting Bulldogs had lost?

"What a difference from last week!" Coach Dad went on.

Mason had to admit that having players who knew how to play had been a definite improvement.

As if reading Mason's thoughts, his dad said, "It was great having a full roster, wasn't it? But you original Bulldogs have also improved by leaps and bounds."

Except for Dylan, who couldn't have made a leap or a bound if his life depended on it.

How could Brody have passed to *Dylan*?

Mason stalked past Brody and his family on the way out to the parking lot. He was so mad that it was better to avoid Brody altogether than to say anything right now.

But Brody caught up with him. "I made us lose," Brody said in a small voice.

Correct!

Mason's dad laid a hand on Brody's slumped shoulder. "I told you all to pass to someone who was open. Dylan was the only one open. Nobody else passed to Dylan for the entire time he was in the game. So you did a kind thing, Brody, to make Dylan feel like he's truly part of our team."

Part of our losing team.

Brody's face brightened. Brody was incapable of staying sad for very long. "I bet we win next time!"

"I bet so, too," Coach Dad said.

Mason didn't say anything.

By the next practice, Mason had forgiven Brody. He and Brody had been best friends since Little Wonders Preschool. Mason wasn't going to stop being best friends with Brody because of one basketball game.

Besides, he wasn't as mad at Brody for a bad pass as for having talked him into playing basketball in the first place, and so far Mason had managed to forgive Brody for that.

This is going to be great! Ha!

The colonial craft that week was writing "mottoes"—inspirational sayings—on parchment with a cartridge pen filled with real ink. Colonial people would have used a quill pen made out of a feather, and they would have made their ink out of crushed berries.

Brody, Nora, and Mason all wrote Ben Franklin sayings.

Brody wrote, "Early to bed, early to rise, makes a man healthy, wealthy, and wise."

Nora wrote, "An ounce of prevention is worth a pound of cure."

Mason wrote, "The worst wheel of a cart makes the most noise."

In Coach Joe's class the worst and noisiest wheel, in Mason's opinion, was Dunk. Dunk's cartridge pen kept blotting. After fifteen minutes, Dunk had ink on his fingers, his nose, even one ear. Sheng laughed at Dunk, and Dunk threatened to smear ink on Sheng. The American Revolution would have broken out all over again if Coach Joe hadn't stepped in to make peace.

On Saturday the Fighting Bulldogs lost their third game in a row, 24–18. Mason had almost scored a basket in the third quarter—the ball had teetered on the rim so long that Brody was already slapping him on the back in congratulation. And then, as if by doomed magic, the ball had refused to go in.

"But look how close we're getting," Coach Dad told the team when they all went out for pizza afterward.

Mason didn't bother to point out that the score had actually been closer the game before, so that technically they were getting worse, not better. He focused on the thought that in a few more weeks, basketball season would be over forever.

Thanksgiving break stretched ahead—long, delicious days with no school, no basketball practice, no basketball game, undisturbed time to hang out with Dog from morning to night.

So long as Dog didn't place any one of his three paws on Mrs. Taylor's lawn.

Mason still had never laid eyes on Mrs. Taylor in the flesh. All he had seen of her was a blurry face at the upstairs window. But he had a good image of her in his mind: toothless—no, maybe with one blackened tooth to make her look like a jack-o'-lantern—a beaked nose—wild, staring eyes—wisps of uncombed white hair—a black peaked hat. . . .

What if Mrs. Taylor had moved next door, not to a kind, gentle, wonderful dog like Dog, but to a barking, biting dog like Dunk's dog, Wolf? Last summer, Wolf had attacked Dog and injured him so badly that Dog had had to go to veterinary urgent care. How would Mrs. Taylor like living next door to a dog like that?

On the afternoon before Thanksgiving, Mason was out in the driveway dribbling up and down with Brody and Dog.

"Are you going somewhere tomorrow? For Thanksgiving?" Brody asked. "I'm going to my grandparents' house."

Mason shook his head. All his relatives lived far away, and no one in his family felt like flying on a busy holiday weekend. So he and his parents and Dog would have their own little Thanksgiving dinner at home. Mason was glad that his mother always made normal holiday food for Thanksgiving—turkey, stuffing, cranberry sauce, sweet potatoes. But then she did strange things with the leftovers. Pakistani turkey curry had been the worst, as Mason recalled.

Brody gave Dog one last hug, and both boys went inside.

The phone was ringing as Mason came into the house. His mother picked it up.

"Who is this, please? . . . Oh, Dunk. . . . How is your finger? . . . I'm glad. . . . Yes, he's right here."

She handed the phone to Mason, who stared at it

106

as if it were under some kind of enchantment. Dunk had come to the house once, to give Dog a present after Dog got hurt by Wolf, but he had never called Mason on the phone.

"Hello?" Mason said cautiously into the receiver.

"My parents made me call," Dunk said, by way of beginning the conversation.

Mason waited to hear exactly why Dunk's parents were making him do this.

"The stupid report? On stupid Ben Franklin? I can't find my stupid library book."

Mason thought about asking, *Whose stupid fault is that?* but he didn't.

"And all the Ben Franklin books are checked out of the public library, and Coach Joe said we have to use real books and not the Internet, and the report is due next week, and I haven't started it yet, so my parents said I have to work on it over the break, and my book disappeared, and they said I have to call someone else who is doing Ben Franklin and borrow their book for a couple of days, and so I called you."

Mason wondered if he should be flattered that Dunk called him and not Nora or Brody.

"I tried to call Nora and Brody, but nobody at their

houses answered the phone," Dunk added. "So can I? Borrow your book? I promise I won't lose it."

Mason hesitated before he replied. Dunk didn't exactly have a stellar track record with library books.

"Okay," he said finally. After all, his report was almost done, so it seemed mean not to loan the book to Dunk.

"Can I come over now and get it?" Dunk asked. "I have to take Wolfie for his walk, anyway."

"Sure," Mason said. "Yeah, come when you walk Wolf." He couldn't bring himself to say "Wolfie."

He could just hand Dunk the book, close the door, and walk away.

Copying Mrs. Taylor, Mason watched from his window for Dunk and Wolf. He heard Wolf barking even before he saw the two of them coming down the street. Dunk was strong, but he was clearly struggling to hold on to Wolf's straining leash.

Mason shrugged on his jacket. Dog jumped up to follow him.

"No, Dog. You have to stay here." Mason wasn't about to allow Wolf to harm Dog again, ever.

Dog gave a little whimper of disappointment, but

then let Mason lead him into the kitchen for a dog biscuit and a hug.

Leaving Dog behind in the kitchen, Mason opened the front door as Dunk and Wolf cut across the lawn to where he was standing.

"Hey, Dunk," Mason said.

"Hey," Dunk said.

Wolf growled a greeting.

"Are you ready for us to cream you again?" Dunk asked.

There were six games in the fall basketball season, and six fourth-grade teams, so the final game was to be a rematch between the Fighting Bulldogs and the Killer Whales.

Mason shrugged. Maybe Dunk didn't yet know that Nora and her friends had joined the team.

"Forty-three to eight," Dunk said. "I mean, I've heard of slaughters, but forty-three to *eight?*"

The pleasant conversation had gone on long enough; it was time for Mason to hand Dunk the library book and send him on his merry way. But busy with attending to Dog, Mason had left the book inside the house on the little table by the front door.

Mason opened the door quietly, hoping Dog wouldn't hear him and come dashing to his side. Luckily, Dog seemed still to be in the kitchen. Dunk crowded in behind Mason, without Wolf, thank goodness.

"There's the book," Mason said, pointing.

Instead of taking the book, Dunk picked up Dog's tennis ball, which lay on the table next to it.

"Is this for your freak dog?" he asked. "How can he catch a ball with only three legs?"

"He can catch better than Wolf!" Mason retorted.

"No, he can't! Wolf can catch ten thousand times better!"

The next thing Mason knew, he was outside again with Dunk and Wolf. Dunk unclipped Wolf from his leash and gave the ball a good hard throw.

Right into the Taylors' yard.

Wolf raced over to get it, as if it had been a freshly killed bird or squirrel.

"Um—" Mason said. "The lady next door? She doesn't like dogs."

But he had to admit he didn't say it very loudly.

Dunk threw the ball even farther the next time.

Again Wolf darted into the Taylors' yard to retrieve the ball, barking his deep, savage bark.

Out of the corner of his eye, Mason glanced toward the Taylors' upstairs window. The curtain was pulled back.

Then, ball in mouth, Wolf apparently remembered that there was some other business he hadn't taken care of yet on his afternoon walk. Still on the Taylors' side of the property line, Wolf carefully squatted and took a nice long time doing a massive poop.

"Do you have a plastic bag with you?" Mason asked Dunk.

Dunk looked puzzled.

"To clean it up? To pick up Wolf's poop?"

Dunk made a retching sound. "Are you kidding? That's disgusting!"

As if it weren't disgusting to let your dog poop on someone else's lawn and then leave it there.

Mission accomplished, Wolf trotted back with the ball and dropped it at Dunk's feet. Dunk threw the ball again, so hard that it landed in the lawn on the other side of the Taylors' house.

"I bet you can't throw as far as I can," Dunk said.

"Wow, Dunk," Mason said. "You *do* throw far. But you'd better be careful. I think there's a law against letting your dog run into other people's yards."

Dunk wouldn't be able to say he hadn't been warned.

"Yeah? What are they going to do about it?" Dunk demanded.

Dunk kept throwing the ball for Wolf, farther and farther. Wolf kept sprinting to get it, barking, barking, barking.

A familiar-looking panel van pulled up in front of Mason's house.

A familiar-looking animal-control officer got out.

"Hey, kids," he said. But he wasn't smiling this time. "I warned you boys to keep your dog off the neighbor's property."

Then he looked more closely at Dunk, who obviously wasn't Brody, and at Wolf, who obviously wasn't Dog.

"My dog is in the house," Mason said innocently. "This is my friend's dog."

Well, my enemy's dog.

"I *told* you to be careful," Mason said to Dunk, trying to make his voice sound irritated.

"Your neighbor reported that not only did you let your dog run wild in her yard with no effort to control him, but you failed to clean up after him," the animal control man continued. "Is that correct?"

"Yes, sir," Mason said, before Dunk could deny it. Now he tried to make his voice sound ashamed. "We're sorry, sir."

"I'm afraid 'sorry' isn't good enough this time," the man said.

From his pocket, he handed Mason a plastic bag.

Mason handed it to Dunk.

Mason was used to picking up dog poop now, but he remembered how sick he had felt the first time he had to do it. And he hadn't even had an animal-control officer watching to make sure he did it correctly.

"I'm going to have to write you a ticket," the man told a green-faced, gagging Dunk, who had returned with a lumpy plastic bag in his hand.

Both boys stood silent as the man took his time filling out the ticket and then handed it to Dunk. "You give that to your parents, you hear?"

"Yes, sir," Dunk mumbled.

It occurred to Mason to be relieved that his own father was out running errands, and his mother was lost in her editing work in her office upstairs at the back of the house.

Then the man got into his van and drove away.

114

"This stinks!" Dunk burst out.

Mason didn't know if Dunk was talking about the poop-filled bag he was holding in one hand or the ticket he was holding in the other hand. Or both.

"My dad is going to kill me!"

Mason gave a small cluck of sympathy.

"Well, Wolf *can* fetch a million times better than Dog! And the Killer Whales *are* going to slaughter you guys again!"

With that, Dunk dropped the bag, clipped Wolf's leash back on, and stalked away.

Mason saw that Dunk had forgotten the bag of dog poop.

And the Ben Franklin library book.

10

Mason stood on the sidewalk, feeling strangely satisfied. Was it Ben Franklin who had said you could kill two birds with one stone?

The saying meant that you could accomplish two things in one fell swoop. For example, even though Mason hadn't planned it that way, you could get even with a nasty old dog hater *and* with a boy who bragged too much about basketball, all by being willing to loan a library book.

When Mason went into the house after tossing the poop bag in the trash, the phone was ringing.

It was far too soon for it to be Dunk, realizing that he had failed to get the one thing that had been the reason for his disastrous visit.

Of course, it could be—

"Mrs. Taylor!" Mason heard his mother say into the phone as she was bustling around in the kitchen getting ready for dinner.

Mason didn't stick around to hear any more. He and Dog fled to the safety of their bedroom.

A few minutes later, his mother pushed open his door. Mason and Dog were lying side by side on Mason's bed.

"Mason," she said in her best disappointed-sounding voice.

"It wasn't my fault! Dunk came to get a book for school, and he had Wolf with him, and you know what Dunk is like! And what Wolf is like! I told him about Mrs. Taylor. But he didn't listen!"

"Yes," his mother said sternly. "I know what Dunk is like, and you do, too. Mrs. Taylor said you played together for half an hour and Wolf repeatedly ran into her yard and did his business on her grass."

"I told Dunk to clean it up!"

"Did *you* clean it up? Dunk and Wolf were here as your guests."

"I didn't invite them. They invited themselves!"

"Mason, Mrs. Taylor was distraught. Do you know what 'distraught' means? Extremely, extremely upset.

She has high blood pressure. She has a heart condition. It is very dangerous for her to get so upset. And I cannot believe that you honestly thought Wolf's behavior wouldn't upset her or that you made any serious effort to stop it."

Mason buried his face in Dog's soft fur. Okay, he did feel awful now. He didn't want to make even a spying dog hater have a heart attack and die. Mason had his faults, but he wasn't a cold-blooded old-lady murderer.

"What should I do?" Mason asked his mom, his voice muffled.

"You need to apologize to Mrs. Taylor."

Mason could write her a note in his best cursive. His mother was big on handwritten thank-you notes for birthday and Christmas presents. Maybe she'd think a handwritten apology note would be a good idea.

"I felt so sorry for the Taylors," she went on, "that I invited them to join us for Thanksgiving dinner tomorrow. So you can apologize to her in person then."

What?

"But—what about Dog? She hates dogs!"

"Dog, I'm afraid, will not be able to have dinner with us. Dog will have to be in the basement."

"But—this is Dog's first Thanksgiving at our house! Dog can't miss Thanksgiving!"

"Mason, from Dog's point of view, Thanksgiving is just another day. You can make it up to him with a nice bone."

"But he'll think he did something bad! And he didn't do anything!"

"I'm well aware that *Dog* didn't do anything. I invited the Taylors for four o'clock," Mason's mother said. She left Mason's room and closed the door firmly behind her.

The roasting turkey smelled wonderful the next day, but Mason couldn't enjoy sniffing its savory aroma. Even though his mother had bought comforting canned cranberry sauce for him—the rest of them were going to have spiced cranberry-raisin chutney— Mason couldn't look forward to any of it.

At four o'clock Dog would be banished to the basement.

At four o'clock Mason would have to make his in-person apology to a mean old dog-hating lady who might die any minute.

Ten minutes before the hour, Mason led poor

Dog down the basement stairs. He gave Dog a huge, smothering hug, together with a nice, fresh dog bone from the butcher.

"Oh, Dog, don't be too sad."

At least, distracted by the bone, Dog didn't pad back up the basement stairs after Mason, so Mason didn't have to shut the basement door right in Dog's sweet face.

Five minutes past the hour, the doorbell rang.

Mason's father answered it. "Come in, come in!"

Mason followed his mother from the kitchen into the living room to greet the Taylors. He knew he had no choice.

His first surprise was that Mrs. Taylor wasn't ugly. She was obviously old, with white hair and finely wrinkled skin, but her hair was attractively styled, and her cheeks were rosy. Her nose was normal-shaped, not hooked or beaked; her eyes were sparkling, not beady.

Mr. Taylor helped her off with her coat and handed it to Mason's dad, along with a bouquet of yellow and orange flowers.

"These are lovely!" Mason's mother said. She carried the flowers into the kitchen to put in a vase as Mason's father hung the coats in the front-hall closet.

"And this is our son, Mason," Mason's father said. "Mason Dixon."

Mrs. Taylor smiled at Mason—smiled at him! "An unusual name," she said.

"Well, my last name is Dixon," Mason's father explained, "and my wife's maiden name is Mason, so we thought it would be fun to combine the two."

At least Mrs. Taylor didn't say, "Oh, *Mason Dixon*! Like the Mason-Dixon Line!" This was apparently a famous line drawn between the North and the South before the Civil War. Grown-ups often tried to explain to Mason about the Mason-Dixon Line, as if a boy named Mason Dixon could have lived almost ten years and never heard this fact about his name.

This was the moment for Mason to make his apology, even though his mother was still in the kitchen. His father could vouch for him afterward.

"I'm sorry," Mason said in a low voice. "About my dog. Well, not about my dog, but the dog yesterday. His name is Wolf, and he's a really bad dog. I know what a bad dog he is because he attacked my dog once and almost killed him."

Mrs. Taylor shuddered. "I could tell he was a very bad dog," she said. "And I have to confess I've always been deathly afraid of dogs. I was bitten once, savagely bitten, when I was a little girl, and I never got over it."

That made some sense. At least there was a reason why Mrs. Taylor felt the way she did.

"Dog—I mean, my dog—would never bite any-one," Mason said.

"He certainly is a better-behaved creature than that other one." Mrs. Taylor shuddered again.

"I was glad Wolf got a ticket," Mason told Mrs. Taylor. "He deserved one. And his owner, Dunk, deserved one, too."

Now Mrs. Taylor's eyes were twinkling, as if she and Mason shared a funny secret.

"You don't care for this boy, I take it? He's not a good friend of yours like the other one. The short boy with the big smile. The one who's so enthusiastic about basketball."

Mason was a bit taken aback by all Mrs. Taylor knew about Brody. She really was a talented spy.

Mason's father led the Taylors over to the couch and offered them a seat. Mason sat down, too. He knew it would be impolite to go downstairs to the basement to be with poor Dog, who had yet to give a single yelp of protest.

"What's your friend's name?" Mrs. Taylor asked.

"Brody. Brody Baxter. We've been best friends since preschool."

He found himself telling Mrs. Taylor about Brody,

and how they shared Dog, and how they were on the same basketball team, and how awful Dunk had acted after their disastrous first game.

Mrs. Taylor clucked sympathetically.

"He sounds like a very poor sport," she commented. "A good sport is a good winner as well as a good loser."

"Win with grace, lose with dignity," Mason said.

"Yes! I'm sure *you're* a very good sport."

Mason thought about how he had accused Dunk's team of bribing Jonah-the-referee. And how mad he had gotten at Brody sometimes for hustling so hard during their one-on-one games. And how he didn't let his fingers actually touch the fingers of anyone on the opposing team for the postgame handshake.

"Not really," he admitted.

"No? Well, I never enjoyed losing myself, I have to say."

"Did *you* play a team sport?"

Mason tried to imagine Mrs. Taylor dribbling down the basketball court to score. He couldn't do it.

"I did. No need to look so astonished. I was a most capable pitcher for a girls' softball team when I was in college. I had a special fastball that the other girls called Kathy's Killerball."

She couldn't be serious.

"Jerry," Mrs. Taylor said to her son. "Look at the boy. He doesn't believe me."

"Kathy's *Killerball?*" Mason asked.

"Batters feared it all over New England," Mrs. Taylor said.

She picked up the hand-knit duck-shaped pillow next to her on the couch. Mason's mother liked to knit odd-shaped objects.

"This is darling!" she exclaimed to Mason's mother. "Did you make it?"

"Yes, I did."

Then the two of them were deep into a conversation about knitting and crocheting and cross-stitch. When were they ever going to get to the dining room and start eating turkey?

"Do you know how many embroidered samplers I've made in my life?" Mrs. Taylor suddenly asked Mason, who had tuned out of the conversation.

From her tone Mason assumed it was a lot.

"Hundreds. You'll have to come over someday and see a few of them. You know, Mason, once upon a time, all children learned how to do cross-stitch, even little boys. Back in colonial times."

"Mason's class at school is studying colonial crafts," Mason's mother said. Her face lit up with a new idea. "Mason, maybe Mrs. Taylor can come in to Coach Joe's class some Thursday afternoon and show you all how to do cross-stitch."

"Cool," Mason said in a strangled voice. Knowing his mom as he did, he was certain she was going to take steps to make sure this really happened.

"I'd love to." Mrs. Taylor beamed at Mason. "I really do like children. I just don't like—"

"Dogs." Mason helped her finish the sentence.

Mrs. Taylor had definitely turned out to be a nicer dog hater than Mason had expected.

11

The first game after Thanksgiving break was against an orange-shirted team that also had girl players on it. Mason named the two girls Braids and Ponytail. Right away he could tell that they were extremely good at basketball. Girls who chose to play on a boys' team obviously were girls to be reckoned with.

Braids had as much hustle as Brody, and in addition she towered over all the other players on both teams. Ponytail was less impressive as a player, but she was plenty good. Plus she was mean. Instead of leaving Dylan alone and pretending he didn't exist, as everyone else had done thus far all season, she called him names.

"Hey, Dork," Mason heard her taunt Dylan. "Why don't you give up and go home?"

Dylan's pale freckled face turned pink.

It was the same thought Mason had had himself a hundred times, but unlike Ponytail, he had never said it out loud.

Mason found himself with a burning desire that the orange team would lose in some particularly horrific and humiliating way, the kind of loss with which he was all too familiar.

Guarding Ponytail, Mason stayed on her so fiercely that she got called for traveling.

Take that, Dorkette!

At the half, the Fighting Bulldogs were behind, but just by one basket.

"I hate them," Mason told Nora, standing behind her in line for the water fountain. "All of them. But especially Ponytail."

"Oh, Mason, it's just a game."

Had Mason himself really ever once thought that games didn't matter? Mason didn't know how Nora could play so intently—half of the Bulldog baskets in the first half were hers—and yet walk off the court with no hard feelings, so calm, so cool, so unflustered. Didn't Nora ever get upset about anything?

"Did you hear how mean she was to Dylan?" Mason persisted.

"That's trash talk. Lots of players do it."

But not to Dylan. It was cruel overkill to point out that Dylan was terrible at basketball.

Mason sat out the third quarter, so he was back in for the fourth, with Brody, Nora, Dylan, and Jeremy. Ponytail was back, too.

"Hey, Midget," she sneered at Brody. "I'm surprised you can even see the ball from down there."

"It's better to have a small body than to have a small brain," Mason shot back.

Nora shot and missed. Both Mason and Ponytail leaped for the rebound, Mason willing his legs to have springs in them so he could soar over the top of her dumb ponytail head.

He did it! He snatched the ball out of the air— yay! Then he landed, hard, on Ponytail's sneaker.

"Ow!" Ponytail yelled. "He fouled me!"

Mason didn't have the strength to yell "Ow!" himself before he crumpled to the hard gymnasium floor.

Fwee! Jonah, back as ref, blew his whistle.

Was it a foul? On him, for landing on Ponytail's big foot? Or on Ponytail, for having her big dumb foot in his way? Right then, with his ankle throbbing, it didn't really matter. Mason lay on the floor, clutching his ankle, moaning.

The rest of the Bulldogs crowded around him. He saw Brody's worried face, Nora's steady eyes. The orange shirts stayed a short distance away, but also stared at him with the fascination people seemed to feel in the face of any hideous disaster—a tornado, a hurricane, an earthquake, an injury to Mason Dixon on the basketball court.

Then Mason's dad was there.

"Are you all right?" he asked Mason, crouching down on the floor and feeling Mason's ankle with his probing fingers.

"No," Mason said.

"I don't feel anything that seems broken. I think you probably rolled it. We'll help you up. But don't put any weight on it until we can get it checked out, okay?"

Jonah assisted Mason's dad in getting Mason to his feet. Mason smelled the sickly sweetness of Jonah's bubblegum breath. Together the two of them half carried Mason to the sidelines. The audience of assembled parents, grandparents, and siblings cheered.

If it had been Brody who had been injured, Brody would have given them a valiant wave and flashed them a brave, hopeful smile.

If it had been Nora who had been injured—but Nora would probably never let herself get injured.

Mason lowered himself onto one of the folding chairs at the edge of the court and buried his head in his hands.

The Bulldogs tied the orange shirts, which was better than losing to them, but not much better.

Mason's mother came to sit beside him. She had gone looking for an ice pack and gotten one from the information desk at the Y. Mason laid it against his swollen ankle, which was propped up on another chair. She put her arm around his shoulder.

"I'm so proud of you," she said.

Proud of him for having a sprained—maybe broken—ankle? If it *was* broken, maybe he could sue Ponytail for a million dollars.

"For working so hard all season," she said. "For giving your best every game. And for being willing to give basketball a try in the first place."

Mason wished he could blame her for making him sign up for basketball, but this time he really had only himself to blame. Anyway, it felt good to have her arm around his shoulder.

As soon as the team handshake was over—at least Mason didn't have to pretend to shake hands with Ponytail—his parents assisted him to the car and drove to a drop-in medical center out on the highway that was open on Saturdays. The doctor who examined him was a small, slim woman who looked like the twin sister of Dog's veterinarian. She sent him down the hall for an X-ray and then agreed with his father in pronouncing it a rolled ankle—sprained, not broken.

"Put ice on it to keep the swelling down, but not for more than fifteen minutes at a time. Take ibuprofen every four hours for pain. And stay off it for a few days," she told Mason and his parents.

"Can he still go to school?" Mason's mother asked after the doctor had finished bandaging the ankle.

"Yes, but no P.E. I'll send a note for his teacher. And no basketball for a while, until it's completely healed."

"How long is a while?" his dad asked. "We have practice on Tuesday, and a game on Saturday, and then the last practice and game of the season the week after that."

The doctor considered this for a minute. "Skip the next practice *and* the next game. Call me then and let me know how the ankle is doing. If you can walk on it without pain, you can try going to the next practice. But if it gets worse at any time, come back and see me."

A few weeks ago Mason would have been thrilled at the thought of missing a whole week of basketball. He would have been glad to miss the whole season, to miss out on basketball completely for the rest of his life. But now it felt strange to think of the Fighting Bulldogs—*his* team—playing without him.

He hoped he would be better in time for the final game, the rematch against Dunk and the Killer Whales—in time to *beat* Dunk and the Killer Whales.

On Tuesday evening, Mason's ankle hurt enough from limping on it all day at school that he stayed home with Dog while his dad and Brody headed off to basketball practice. He could picture Brody's skip of enthusiasm as they neared the school; Brody was the only fourth-grade boy Mason knew who was actually capable of skipping. Mason could picture the arrival of the others, the warm-up stretches, the passing and shooting drills, the three-on-three.

At least his mother read to him as he lay on

the couch with his throbbing ankle and Dog on the floor listening, too. She liked to read him all the old-fashioned books she had loved when she was a little girl. Right now they were reading *Peter Pan*, the original book, not the Disney version, so that helped pass the time, even though Mason found his thoughts straying from Peter and Wendy to Brody and Nora.

"So how was it?" Mason asked as soon as his dad came through the door at eight-thirty.

"Great! We're going to win a game one of these days, mark my words."

Mason was glad for his dad's report, though he wondered if the team should have moped a bit over the absence of their injured comrade.

"But everyone missed you," his dad said then.

Was his dad saying it just to be nice?

"Did they?"

"Every time Brody made a good shot, he dedicated it to you. Really. He said, 'That one was for Mason.'"

Mason felt himself beaming as broadly as Brody himself would have done.

Thursday was the day that Mrs. Taylor appeared in Coach Joe's class to show the students how to make cross-stitch samplers. Mason's mother came in with Mrs. Taylor, to help her find the room and to serve as her cross-stitch-teaching assistant.

The previous week had been candle dipping. The custodian hadn't yet gotten out all of the wax that Dunk had dripped onto the carpet.

"Hello, Mason! Hello, Brody!" Mrs. Taylor greeted the two of them by name, even though she had never met Brody before. Brody's eyes widened with surprise, even though Mason had told him all about Thanksgiving dinner.

Mason noticed that Mrs. Taylor didn't say, "Hi, Dunk," even though she had to have been able to pick him out after her fateful spying that day. So Mrs. Taylor knew who Dunk was. But Dunk didn't know who Mrs. Taylor was.

Each student was given a square of plain white fabric printed with a heart made out of little *x*'s.

"I don't want to sew a heart," Dunk said. "Hearts are for girls."

Then Dunk apparently remembered that he didn't want to sew *anything*.

"*Sewing* is for girls," he added.

"Dunk," Coach Joe said pleasantly.

"It's true that in colonial times the women of the house did most of the sewing and cooking," Mrs. Taylor said. "But a man would have been embarrassed indeed at not being able to do some simple sewing, at least enough to fasten on a button to keep his britches from falling down."

The class laughed. Mason felt proud of Mrs. Taylor. Every student was then given a needle.

Mason wondered if this craft was going to turn out to be a bad idea. Needles were sharp. What if Dunk decided to test the sharpness of his needle on the hand of the boy sitting next to him?

Instead, Dunk promptly lost his needle. It rolled off his desk and onto the floor, and the gray carpet was needle-colored enough that Dunk couldn't find it. The boy sitting next to him couldn't find it either, although why that boy wanted to find it Mason wasn't quite sure.

Just as Mrs. Taylor was about to hand Dunk a new needle, Nora spied the first one and gave it back to Dunk.

Threading the needles with a special kind of thread called embroidery floss took a few more minutes, and then learning how to tie a knot at the end of the thread. Mason marveled at the patience of co-lonial people.

Finally the students started sewing, making one little stitch on each printed *x*, then another stitch to complete the *x*.

"No, Dunk," Mason heard Mrs. Taylor say, "you need to have your knot on the back of your sampler. You want the messy side of your sampler to be the *back*."

She helped Dunk rip out what he had done so far and start again.

"No, Dunk. You need to keep your stitches small. And neat. Like this."

Brody's heart was almost done. Nora had completed her heart several minutes ago.

"Don't jab with the needle," Mrs. Taylor told Dunk. "Just pull the thread through gently."

Mason had only finished six x's on his heart; he was spending too much time watching Dunk with Mrs. Taylor.

"Dunk, if you keep jabbing your needle that way, you're going to stab your—"

A wail went up from Dunk's table.

"—finger," Mrs. Taylor said.

"It's bleeding! My finger's bleeding!"

"Who are you going to give your heart to?" Brody asked Mason. "I'm going to frame mine and give it to Albert." Albert was Brody's pet goldfish. "I'm going to hang it in my room right over his bowl."

"I don't think anyone's going to want mine," Mason said. His thread kept bunching and tangling, and he couldn't make his stitches small and neat like Brody's and Nora's.

"Now there's blood in my heart!" Dunk bellowed.

As the end of the sewing session drew near, Mason's heart still had a long way to go.

"You can finish these up at home, if you need to," Mrs. Taylor said. "You may keep the needle and take it with you."

"Do finish them," Coach Joe said. "Remember, we're having our Colonial School Day next week. We'll want to have all your crafts on display."

However bad Mason's botched heart looked, Mason was sure Dunk's bloodstained heart looked even worse.

"No, Dunk," Mrs. Taylor said. "Here, put your needle in your sampler *this* way, so you don't lose it."

Again.

"Or stab yourself."

Again.

"Oh, and Dunk?" Mason heard her say, in a lower voice this time, so low that he could only hear it because he was straining his ears to listen.

"What?" Dunk asked sullenly.

"Keep your dog off my lawn. Do you hear?"

Then, with a warm smile at the class, Mrs. Taylor gathered up her sewing supplies and sailed out the door, followed by Mason's mother, who turned and gave Mason one last smile before she went.

12

The second Saturday in December, from eleven a.m. to noon, was the hour when Mason officially learned how to cheer. Loudly. Embarrassingly. With all his heart. Stuck in his folding chair at the edge of the basketball court, it was the only thing he could do to help the Fighting Bulldogs win.

"Aw!" he moaned in disgust when Jonah called a foul against Kevin.

"Yes!" he shouted in triumph when Brody sank a great three-point shot to give the Bulldogs a 17–14 lead at the half. Despite his bandaged ankle, Mason couldn't stop himself from jumping to his feet and doing his own version of a happy dance.

Mason hobbled out to join the halftime huddle.

Injured or non-injured, playing or not playing, he was still part of the team.

Coach Dad gave his best pep talk yet. Mason had noticed that his dad wasn't relying on the coaching book so much anymore; he had even gone back to struggling with sudoku puzzles at the breakfast table.

"We can win this one," Coach Dad said, "but only if we go out there not as Kevin, Jeremy, Matt, Brody, Dylan, Nora, Elise, Amy, and Tamara—and Mason—but as the Fighting Bulldogs."

Mason was glad that his father had remembered to add his name to the list.

And the Bulldogs did win, 26–24.

Mason was hoarse from screaming.

But why, oh why, couldn't he have been out there playing, too? It was a Bulldogs victory, yes, the team's first win, but despite his dad's great speech, it hadn't been *Mason's* victory. Unless yelling until you had a sore throat counted.

Which it sort of did.

But sort of didn't.

Wednesday evening was the Plainfield Platters' winter holiday concert: songs about dreidels and Santa and snowmen and sleigh rides, even though it hadn't snowed since that early snow at the end of October, when the new-fallen snow in the Taylors' yard had been marred by Dog's footprints.

Nowadays, when Mason saw Mrs. Taylor looking out from her upstairs window, he waved. He thought he could see her waving back.

But he still kept Dog out of her yard.

During the Platters concert, Mason was one of the kids who rang a handbell for "Silver Bells," which he knew was a big thrill for his mother. Brody wore an elf costume for "Santa Claus Is Coming to Town," which Mason knew was a big thrill for Brody. Puff the Plainfield Dragon was at the concert, looking festive in a Santa cap, which was a big thrill for the little kids in the audience. Mason got through the concert without any disastrous moments; that wasn't exactly a big thrill for him, but it was definitely a relief.

Then it was Thursday, another day to gladden the heart of Brody: Colonial School Day for Coach Joe's class.

Mason wore his regular clothes—jeans and a plain, solid-colored T-shirt. At least it was more colonial than a T-shirt from Disney World, not that

Mason owned such a thing. Brody wore jeans, too, with a button-down shirt and his three-cornered hat from Philadelphia.

Nora wore a long, old-fashioned-looking cotton dress and a sunbonnet, her straight dark hair fashioned in two neat braids, tied with hair ribbons.

"I didn't think you'd wear a dress," Mason said.

"You didn't think I'd be on your basketball team, either," Nora said.

To begin the school day, Coach Joe clanged a large bell set on his desk. He was dressed in a full eighteenth-century outfit, complete with breeches that fastened under his knees, long stockings, buckled shoes, and a ruffled shirt.

"Good morning, boys and girls," Coach Joe said in a formal-sounding way.

"Good morning, Master Joseph!" the class chorused.

On each desk sat a small wooden-edged slate, a stick of chalk, and a scrap of rag for an eraser.

For math, the pupils wrote their sums on their slates. Master Joseph called on each student to stand up in turn by the side of his or her desk to recite. Everyone recited correctly, for in the corner of the room now stood a wooden stool crowned by a tall paper cone: the dreaded dunce cap.

Then Dunk, dressed in his ordinary clothes, got an easy answer wrong. Mason knew he had done it on purpose, to see if Master Joseph would really send him into the corner. Besides, Colonial School Day wouldn't be fun if no one sat in the corner playing the role of the dunce.

"Master Duncan, did you study your sums last night?" Master Joseph asked with mock sternness.

"No," Dunk said. For good measure, he stuck out his tongue.

"Master Duncan, I'm afraid I must punish you. I will not rap your knuckles with my ruler—today— but I will send you to the corner to sit on the dunce stool in disgrace."

Laughing, Dunk swaggered over to the stool and hopped up on it so energetically that the stool tipped over, with Dunk upon it, sending Dunk sprawling onto the floor.

"Master Duncan," Master Joseph said, "pray be more careful."

Dunk rubbed his elbow, righted the stool, and climbed back onto it, less cheerfully this time.

"The cap, Master Duncan," Master Joseph instructed. He didn't chuckle as he said it. He made it sound like a real punishment in a real colonial school.

Scowling now, Dunk jerked the cap onto his head. The class started laughing. Dunk did look ridiculous sitting there perched on the stool with his peaked paper cap like a white witch's hat without a brim.

Master Joseph called on the next student. "Emma Averill, what is seven times forty-three?"

"Three hundred and one," Emma answered correctly, but the sound of her answer was drowned out by Brody's friend Sheng, calling out, "Master Joseph, Dunk took off his dunce's cap."

The whole class turned toward Dunk. Dunk had not only taken off the dunce cap, he had thrown it onto the floor.

"Master Duncan," Master Joseph said, his voice gentle now, "you may go back to your seat."

"Make someone else wear the dunce cap!" Dunk burst out as he jumped down from the tall stool. He looked around the room wildly, but everyone else was sitting properly in place, backs erect, slates at the ready.

Dunk's glance fell on Mason.

"Make *him* wear the dunce cap. Mason Dixon. He got me and Wolf in trouble with that cross-stitch lady, and we got a ticket, and it was for fifty dollars, and I told my mother but now my father found out, and he might make me quit basketball, and the last game of the season is this Saturday, and it's against *his* team, and I think he did it just to get even for the first game, but it wasn't my fault that he stinks!"

150

"Team," Coach Joe said, using his Coach Joe voice and not his Master Joseph voice. "I think maybe we're finding out why modern-day schools don't use a dunce cap anymore. It doesn't make the person wearing it feel very good, does it, even when it's done in fun, as it was supposed to be today. So I, Master Joseph"—Coach Joe used his colonial teacher voice again—"hereby decree: no more dunce caps in Master Joseph's school."

Dunk stood sulking, looking almost as upset as when he had smashed his finger with the hammer on punched-tin-lantern day or stuck his finger with the needle on cross-stitch-sampler day.

"Master Duncan," Master Joseph said, "will you do us the honor of taking our dunce cap and ripping it up for us?"

This was plainly an invitation Dunk couldn't resist.

Still glaring at Mason, Dunk grabbed the paper cap off the floor where he had hurled it and began tearing it into pieces, until the floor was littered with torn scraps of dunce cap.

Mason knew that this was what Dunk wanted the Killer Whales to do to the Fighting Bulldogs on Saturday. And Saturday was just two days away.

When it was time for recess, Coach Joe asked Mason and Dunk to wait for a minute.

Uh-oh.

"Boys," Coach Joe said when the two of them were standing in front of his desk. "I thought we agreed that what happens on the basketball court stays on the basketball court."

Mason felt his own face reflecting Dunk's scowl. *Dunk* was the one who kept on gloating about his team; he, Mason, hadn't said anything more against the Killer Whales, though he had to admit that he *thought* things all the time.

"Boys. Don't you think I care about sports? Don't you think I love just about every game that there is?"

Mason was willing to concede that a teacher who called himself Coach Joe was fond of sports.

"But—I want you to repeat this after me—sports are not everything," Coach Joe said.

"Sports are not everything," Mason and Dunk muttered.

"Basketball is just a game," Coach Joe said.

"Basketball is just a game," Mason and Dunk repeated.

"Play your best. Play to win. Then shake hands and be friends again."

But we aren't friends, Mason wanted to say. *We'll never be friends.*

"Okay, now let's see you shake hands," Coach Joe instructed.

With Coach Joe watching so closely, Mason couldn't do his usual handshake-without-touching-hands trick. He shook Dunk's hand.

But then, on his way to recess, he stopped in the boys' room and washed his hand where Dunk had touched it.

13

"Are you sure you don't want scrambled eggs this morning?" Mason's mother asked as Mason and his dad came to the breakfast table Saturday morning. "Some protein? Before the big game?"

Mason rolled his eyes at his dad as he poured his plain Cheerios into his plain white bowl.

The coaching book was back on the breakfast table again—not open to be read, but apparently just there as a good-luck charm.

Mason could use all the luck he could get. At least his ankle was healed enough that he could play; he had had to miss practice again on Tuesday night.

Mason's family arrived at the Y so early that the previous game was only at halftime: Ponytail's team playing against the team that the Bulldogs, without

Mason, had beaten last weekend. Mason hoped Ponytail's team would lose, but he couldn't spend time thinking about it. His mind was full of other things.

Would Dunk be there? It wouldn't be the same beating the Killer Whales if Dunk's dad made good on his threat to make Dunk quit the team. This last game had to be a showdown between the two of them.

Last night Mason's mother had read him the scene of Peter Pan's final showdown with Captain Hook, where Peter swore his terrible oath, "Hook or me this time," and sent Captain Hook to his death at the jaws of the waiting crocodile.

Then Mason saw a familiar, swaggering, blue-shirted form across the gym. His heart swelled with mingled dread and relief.

Dunk or me this time.

The other game ended: Ponytail's team lost 20–18.

A good omen?

In the few minutes between the two games, Jonah, wearing his referee's shirt, came up to Mason and his dad.

"Ankle okay?" Jonah asked.

Mason was too surprised to answer. He hadn't thought of Jonah as a person who might ask him a friendly question, but as a corrupt gum chewer paid off by the other team.

"Much better," Mason's dad answered for him. "Thanks for asking."

Jonah gave Mason a friendly smile.

Mason found himself smiling back.

The game began. Mason didn't start; he saw that Dunk didn't start either. Mason had decided that he liked going in later, anyway, when the stakes were higher and every basket counted more.

Brody was in, out-hustling all his past hustle, which was saying a lot. He was a little yellow whirlwind—grabbing the ball right out of a befuddled Whale's grip, taking it down the court, passing it to Kevin, who passed it to Amy, who passed it back to Brody, who shot a perfect layup and scored.

Maybe it *was* good in basketball to be short.

Mason went in for the second quarter, with Nora and Dylan. Sometime between the previous game and this one, Dylan seemed to have gotten a clue. He waved his hands in a Whale's face as if he finally understood that the point of guarding was to keep the other kid from scoring, as opposed to making random motions in the air. Dylan even caught the ball once, from a well-timed pass by Nora, and passed it on to Mason—the first successful pass of Dylan's life.

Was Mason within scoring range? He took a chance and sent the ball flying toward the backboard; it fell through the hoop with a sweet, satisfying swish of success, his first basket in a real game.

His ankle still hurt some when he landed on it. He didn't care.

At the half, the score was tied 13–13.

Sweat trickled down Mason's forehead as he listened to Coach Dad's halftime speech in the huddle.

"We have two quarters left," his dad said. "Twelve minutes left of our first season playing together as a team. I want us to win. But more than that, I want us to play like winners. And that means playing with respect for one another and for the other team. Playing with sportsmanship. That's what I care about more than anything. And, team, that's how you have been playing. And I'm proud of all of you."

Mason felt his dad's eyes fall on him.

And he knew his dad was proud of him, Mason.

When Mason went in for the final quarter, with Nora, Brody, Amy, and Jeremy, the score was 17–15, with the Bulldogs in the lead—too close for comfort. Dunk was back in as well.

Dunk or me this time.

Dunk had the ball and was dribbling fiercely down the court. Brody leaped in front of Dunk. Brody went down.

Fwee! Jonah blew his whistle.

Mason knew the foul was Brody's, and that Dunk had been going so fast he really had no choice but to mow Brody down. But Brody was the one on the floor, whimpering with pain, clutching not his ankle but his left arm, which had taken the brunt of the impact from his fall.

Once again, Mason's dad was there, feeling Brody's arm for a possible fracture. Fleetingly, Mason wondered how his dad had learned how to do this with so much calm authority. Did the coaching book have a chapter on first aid?

"I think it's okay," Coach Dad said, "but you need to catch your breath, Brody. That was a hard fall you took just now."

Dylan went in for Brody.

Great.

Jonah called a blocking foul against Brody, even

though Mason thought that trading Brody for Dylan was already punishment enough for the Bulldogs.

"He should have called a charging foul against Dunk!" Jeremy complained to Mason. "Dunk knocked Brody down!"

Mason didn't want to point out that Brody had actually been the one in the wrong, blocking Dunk's way.

"Is that ref blind?" Jeremy went on. "Or was he bribed?"

Oh, get over it, Mason thought.

Did *he* use to sound that way?

Dunk was given a free throw. The players on both teams lined up on each side of the key as Dunk took his place.

Looking nervous, Dunk bounced the ball twice.

"Dunk the Dunce!" Jeremy whispered as Dunk readied himself to shoot, loud enough for Dunk to hear, but not loud enough for Jonah-the-ref to hear.

Dunk reddened.

Apparently pleased with this insult, Jeremy used it again: "Dunk the Dunce!"

"Stop it," Mason hissed to Jeremy, loudly.

After all, if what happened on the basketball court

should stay on the basketball court, what happened at school should stay at school.

Jeremy stared at Mason, but fell silent.

Dunk gave Mason a look he couldn't quite read— was it gratitude? Then Dunk shot and scored.

17–16.

Nora scored next: 19–16, Fighting Bulldogs.

The Killer Whales scored: 19–18, Fighting Bull-dogs. Again just one point ahead.

Twenty seconds.

The Bulldogs had the ball now. Amy was dribbling down the court when Dylan fell, for no reason that Mason could see. Maybe now someone else could go in for Dylan?

Coach Dad called a time-out. Apparently Dylan had just tripped on his shoelaces and was fine.

Oh, well.

"Twenty seconds," Coach Dad reminded the team as they headed back onto the court, as if they needed a reminder.

Mason never would have guessed that a mere twenty seconds could count so much.

From the sidelines, he tossed the ball in to Nora, who pelted down the court with it in her usual expert, completely controlled way, eyes unwaveringly on the basket.

"Nora!" Mason yelled, but she didn't stop.

She shot. She scored.

Or would have scored.

Except that Nora had somehow—how could this be?—gone down the court in the wrong direction and shot into the wrong basket.

Nora Alpers, who never made a mistake, had just made the most terrible mistake possible, at the most terrible time possible.

20–19, Whales.

Mason jogged over to Nora as she stood frozen beneath the basket, obviously now realizing what she had done, stunned with shame, paralyzed with disbelief.

He had to say something, but what?

"If we lose, it's my fault," she whispered.

"Before you joined the team, we were losing forty-three to eight!"

She still stood there, even though Jonah-the-ref was obviously waiting for play to resume.

"Nora," Mason said. "It's only a game."

Then Nora gave a shaky grin.

The ball still belonged to the Bulldogs. Nora threw it in to Mason. Even though the clock was ticking down to a Bulldogs defeat, Mason dribbled as calmly as he could, trying to assess his options, none of which were good. This was one chance he couldn't afford to blow.

Amy, Nora, and Jeremy were heavily guarded, though Jeremy kept signaling to Mason to pass to him. Jeremy was probably Mason's best bet.

No one was guarding Dylan. The Killer Whales still apparently thought of Dylan as a non-player who could be safely ignored.

"Mason!" Nora called to him. "Dylan's open!"

Was Dylan open worse than another player not open?

Twelve seconds.

Was Nora wrong better than anybody else right?

Nora had just been stupendously wrong about something.

But the answer to the question, in Mason's mind, was still yes.

Mason passed to Dylan.

Dylan caught the ball.

Dylan dribbled toward the hoop.

Dylan stopped and looked around with utter panic and desperation.

Was Dylan going to start dribbling again and be called on a double dribble?

"Shoot, Dylan!" Nora called to him.

Dylan shot.

The ball teetered on the rim.

The ball went in.

Fwee! Jonah blew his whistle, ending the game. The game that the Fighting Bulldogs had just won, 21–20, against the Killer Whales.

Brody was back on the court, hugging Mason, and Mason was hugging Brody. Everyone pounded Dylan on the back, Mason pounding harder than anyone.

"You did it! Dylan, you did it!" he heard himself shouting.

Nora, usually so calm, was part of the hug, and Coach Dad was, too.

In his mind, Mason hugged his mom and Coach Joe and Dog, of course—even Mrs. Taylor.

It was time for the team handshake.

Mason touched everybody's hand this time—especially Dunk's.

Maybe next season—he knew there would be a

next season—he'd be able to get better at losing with dignity, but for now it was great—terrific! astonishing! wonderful!—to be able to win with grace.

Mason grinned at Brody—a grin big enough to match the grin that Brody grinned back.

ACKNOWLEDGMENTS

It is such a pleasure to be able to thank some of the wonderful, brilliant, creative people who helped bring this book into being: my longtime Boulder writing group (Marie DesJardin, Mary Peace Finley, Ann Whitehead Nagda, Leslie O'Kane, Phyllis Perry, and Elizabeth Wrenn); my unfailingly insightful and encouraging editor, Nancy Hinkel; my wise and caring agent, Stephen Fraser; consistently helpful Jeremy Medina; magnificently sharp-eyed copy editors Janet Frick and Artie Bennett; Guy Francis for his funny, tender pictures; and Sarah Hokanson for her appealing book design. And a special thank-you to Cory Aragon, who read all the basketball scenes and taught me the difference between a blocking foul and a charging foul, and so much more.

CLAUDIA MILLS is the author of over forty books for young readers, including *Mason Dixon: Pet Disasters* and *Mason Dixon: Fourth-Grade Disasters*. She is terrible at all sports, especially basketball, as she is not tall, is not very coordinated, and has no hustle. So instead she curls up with her cat, Snickers, on her couch at home in Boulder, Colorado, drinking hot chocolate and writing. Visit Claudia at claudiamillsauthor.com.